North of the Line

This direct sequel to *The Lawmen* sees Deputy United States Marshal Jesse Bronson sent north of the line into Canada, to assist with the capture of two highly dangerous American outlaws. Brin Carson and Vern Hatcher have joined up with a gang of ruthless Metis half-breeds led by Gabriel Dumont. Their joint aim is to lucratively target the Canadian Pacific Railroad, who have not experienced any train robberies before. To his surprise, Bronson discovers that he is again to be partnered with Samuel Bairstow of the Northwest Mounted Police. And thanks to Dumont's brutality, Bairstow has a personal score to settle that could jeopardise the whole mission.

North of the Line

Paul Bedford

A Black Horse Western

ROBERT HALE

© Paul Bedford 2019
First published in Great Britain 2019

ISBN 978-0-7198-2937-6

The Crowood Press
The Stable Block
Crowood Lane
Ramsbury
Marlborough
Wiltshire SN8 2HR

www.bhwesterns.com

Robert Hale is an imprint
of The Crowood Press

Typeset by
Derek Doyle & Associates, Shaw Heath
Printed and bound in Great Britain by
4Bind Ltd, Stevenage, SG1 2XT

*In memory of my mother, Eileen Winifred (1925-2014),
who enjoyed her visit to Canada and thankfully
didn't come to grief there . . . unlike many of
the characters in this book!*

CHAPTER ONE

Nine horses were ground tethered with iron picket pins close to the tracks. Yet only eight men were visible as they laboured hard at their task ... or rather six of them did. The other two, both wearing distinctive 'Boss of the Plains' hats, provided the tools and the basic instructions that they made great play of imparting.

'First off,' one of them remarked with studied significance, 'The fishplates connecting one of these here rails with the other have to be unbolted, an' this be the tool that'll do it.' So saying, the speaker somewhat exaggeratedly handed over a long-handled running spanner.

Since two rails were to be entirely removed, this job had to be carried out four times. Then twenty retaining spikes had to be levered out of the wooden crossties, this time with crowbars supplied by the pair of work shy Americans. Only then could the thirty-foot long rails be lifted out of line. Weighing six hundred pounds each, that was no easy undertaking for wiry individuals unused to this kind of heavy manual work.

Of course it would have been far easier just to block the track with a fallen tree, but on Saskatchewan's exposed southern plains such things were a rarity. As were railroad hold-ups, although that was soon to change. As the half-dozen sweating half-breeds gratefully released the second rail onto the ground next to the abruptly redundant track ballast, one of their 'instructors' levelled his draw-tube spyglass. Squinting against the dazzling sunlight, he peered back along the empty track. For a long moment, all he could make out was the shimmering heat haze. Then he chuckled. The unmistakeable smudge of smoke on the eastern horizon meant that they wouldn't have much longer to wait.

'Hot dang,' he exclaimed. 'Trains actually run on time up here. I thought you Canadians was only just out of the Stone Age.'

One of the indigenous occupants of the province glared at him. 'We're Metis, not Canadians. Those *cochons* back east want to control all this land and make it their own, but their ways aren't our ways.'

The American gazed at him distractedly. 'Yeah, well, now's your chance to bite back, and make some dollar into the bargain. When that train gets here, you fellas tackle the boxcar. Vern an' me will handle the crew and passengers. With Dumont already on board, the whole thing should be a piece of piss!'

*

Kirsty Bairstow was a fine-looking brunette, with a good complexion and all her own teeth. Always something of a tomboy, she preferred to wear denim pants, rather than the more feminine but constricting dresses favoured by most of her sex. In her case, such male attire tended to emphasize her enviable figure. These combined attributes oftentimes attracted enthusiastic male attention, but she had the sense to recognize her good fortune and mostly accepted it with easy grace. Yet *this* encounter was shaping up to be something entirely different!

Despite there being many empty seats in her particular railroad carriage, her unwanted admirer had placed himself directly opposite, with his back to the engine. With both of them having boarded the westbound train in Regina, it was therefore painfully obvious that he had taken a shine to the apparently unaccompanied young woman. There were two particular problems with that.

Even if she hadn't been married, which she was, his very appearance made her flesh crawl with distaste. He was short and squat, with sallow features and distinctive smallpox scars. And what made it even worse was that Kirsty knew exactly *what* he was. Less than two years earlier, her beloved father, Kirk, had been murdered by others of his kind, south of the border in the Territory of Montana.

The Metis leered at her suggestively, before making his opening gambit. 'Perhaps you'd be more comfortable over here, *leetle* lady,' he suggested, in heavily accented English, as he patted the seat next to him. Then, after pausing for effect, the French-Canadian half-breed allowed his tongue to protrude lewdly, before licking his lips. He then favoured her with a thoroughly intimidating stare. His apparent intention was to inspire fear, followed by acquiescence. Such tactics had succeeded many times before, and would surely do so again. 'Do not be afraid, *ma Cherie*. I intend merely to pass the time with you, *oui?*' With that, he again patted the wooden bench seat, effectively issuing a summons.

Kirsty took in all this and more, because she was no stranger to life *and* death on the frontier. She observed the holstered revolver at his waist, the Winchester Repeater at his side, and the skinning knife protruding from his right boot. And yes, she *was* afraid, but she also possessed grit. Unless this scoundrel literally attempted to rape her, she knew that it was unlikely that any of her few fellow travellers would come to her aid. They were mostly just simple settlers on their way to claim land offered free of charge by the government in Ottawa. But if she could fend him off until the Canadian Pacific train had covered the mere forty miles to her destination, then she would be safe.

Boldly staring back at him, Kirsty shook her head emphatically. 'My *husband* is waiting for me at Moose Jaw. It would behove you to keep well clear of him, mister. He is a *Mounted Policeman!*'

The Metis's eyes widened theatrically. The obvious threat completely failed to move him, because he had no intention of still being on the train when it did finally arrive at Moose Jaw. 'Be . . . beho . . . *quoi?* I ain't never heard such as that before,' he remarked playfully.

'Well maybe you should have attended school. Or don't your kind bother with education?' she retorted unwisely, forgetting that such a man might be overly touchy about pretty much anything.

The stinging open-handed blow across the face took her completely by surprise. Involuntary tears flooded into her eyes as she recoiled under the force. Dimly, Kirsty perceived her assailant's brutalised features suddenly looming uncomfortably close to her. He had risen to his feet, and was now crouching in front of her like a great bird of prey.

'Don't ever sass me, *Cherie!*' he hissed. 'I have a . . . *treatment* for those that displease me.'

His sour breath wafted over her, but pressed against the seat back as she was, there was no escape from it. Then his right hand caressed her inner right thigh, and pain was replaced by anger. With all her strength, and without regard for the consequences, she slammed her left leg up into his unprotected groin. A huge vein bulged on his forehead, and his eyes seemed to expand almost comically. Yet there would be nothing funny about the eventual retribution. Even as he collapsed to his knees, Kirsty knew that she had to seek help.

Leaping to her feet, she barged him out of the way and turned to look at her immediate travelling companions. They amounted to three farming families, who were now peering over at her section of

11

the carriage with surprise and alarm. None of them displayed any inclination to get involved, which was undoubtedly very sensible. They very likely had little or no experience of gunplay, and it would almost certainly need that and more to stop the enraged Metis.

At the rear of the train was a mysteriously sealed boxcar that may or may not have contained Canadian Pacific employees. It was too much of a gamble. Instinctively, she decided to make for the engine, where the crew at least would be duty bound to assist her. There was another carriage between her and it. That would at least provide some space, and it might even contain some rather more inspiring passengers from whom she could seek help. Mind made up, she turned for the door. At that instant, a vicelike grip enveloped her left ankle.

Aghast at his unexpected recovery, Kirsty twisted around and kicked out viciously. The half-breed was still on his knees, so it was a simple matter to aim at his unprotected face. Again and again she lashed out, and each blow drew blood. With his groin still on fire, he finally could take no more. The clawed fingers fell away and she was free ... but for how long?

Racing for the door, the desperate fugitive yanked it open. Stepping out onto the exposed platform, she momentarily contemplated throwing herself off the train, but self-preservation stopped her. It was moving too fast, and the prospect of a broken neck just didn't appeal. Jumping across the gap between one swaying carriage and the next, she heaved open another door and plunged inside.

'Holy shit!' The engineer couldn't believe his eyes. Because their progress across the seemingly endless plains didn't demand his constant attention, he'd taken time away from his position by the controls to share a ribald joke with the sweating fireman. What he now saw meant that his lapse of duty could quite literally be the death of them, passengers and all. The fact that there was an unknown band of men lurking nearby in such a remote area was cause for concern, but it was the removal of a section of track that really had his pulse racing.

'Brace yourself,' he hollered at his startled companion on the footplate. Any thought of a smooth reduction in speed to avoid injury to the passengers was futile. Ignoring normal procedure, the frantic engineer slammed the regulator valve down and applied the steam brake fully. Then, as the sound of tortured metal reached his ears, he repeatedly sounded the whistle, out of naive concern for those fellows waiting down the track. In his fevered state, it never occurred to him that they might actually be responsible for his terrifying predicament.

Kirsty had barely entered the carriage when the floor lurched beneath her and she was flung forwards. As other passengers and possessions collided, she just managed to seize hold of a seat back and so remain upright. Wheels screeched on the track beneath her as the train continued to slow down far more force-fully than usual. Instinctively she glanced back through the glass panel in the door, and her heart sank at the sight of her bloodied persecutor stagger-ing onto the platform outside. He had to possess the constitution of an ox to be back on his feet so rapidly.

Releasing her hold, Kirsty ran for the next door. Beyond that lay the high-backed tender and then the engine with its crew of two. They at least should be prepared to help her . . . if she could reach them.

As it happened, her arrival on the last platform coincided with the train finally coming to a shudder-ing halt. That provided her with an easy option. Whatever the reason for the unscheduled stop, she could just drop to the ground and run to safety. But then, quite unexpectedly, a man appeared at the foot of the steps wearing a wide-brimmed range hat. Any relief that she might have felt was banished by the sudden presence of a six-gun pointing directly at her face.

'Whoa there, little lady,' he commanded with more than a hint of menace. 'I didn't say anyone could leave!'

The crewmen stared at the grim-faced strangers with baffled incomprehension. Their engine had come to a stop mere feet from the missing stretch of track. The fact that a train robbery was in progress simply hadn't occurred to them, because as of that year 1887 there had, to their knowledge, never been one in Canada before. Then, at the sight of so many weapons, the harsh reality suddenly began to dawn on them. It was the soot-covered fireman who reacted first.

Tucked away near the coal tender was a Colt Army that he kept for snakes and such. Common sense should have told him that he didn't really stand a chance, but some foolish notion made him try anyway. As the revolver appeared in his right hand, one of the Americans swiftly drew a bead on his chest and fired first. With a howl of pain, the stricken fireman staggered back a pace, before collapsing to his knees on the footplate. As blood erupted from the mortal wound, his companion stared at him in wide-eyed shock.

'Greetings from the good ole U S of A,' the killer remarked laconically. 'He must have thought it was a good day to die.'

'Why did you have to kill him, for Christ sake?' demanded the horrified engineer. 'He's got two children.'

'He called it when he reached for that hog leg,' replied the other man dismissively. 'And you'll be next if you go on the prod. Now get down out of that cab and sit on your hands. Pronto!'

Even as the now thoroughly cowed railroad employee descended to the ground reluctantly, the crowbar-wielding Metis advanced eagerly on the boxcar. What stopped the six of them in their tracks was firstly the sight of a highly attractive young woman on the platform of the first carriage. She alone was worth a second look, but then one of their own kind burst through the doorway behind her. His battered features were coated in blood, and he was clearly beside himself with rage.

The American who was covering her with his revolver glanced over at the new arrival with some surprise. Slowly, a lopsided smile appeared on his face. 'Well, hell, Gabriel. Looks like you've done tangled with a grizzly. Surely you ain't been bested by this little peach!'

Wordlessly, the other man spat a mouthful of blood into Kirsty's hair and then unleashed a backhanded slap that sent her tumbling off the platform and down to the hard ground. Only then did he offer a response. 'She took me unawares, but it won't happen again. I'll be the only one doing the taking from now on. Not that it's any of your concern, Carson.'

Brin Carson shrugged and turned away. Since it appeared that he no longer had first claim on the girl, his interest had waned abruptly. She *was* undeniably attractive, but he and his partner, Vern Hatcher, had come north for the money. If they wanted a poke, then there would likely be plenty of willing whores in Regina for men with an abundance of cash in their pockets. 'Enjoy,' he remarked, and moved off towards the boxcar. To his certain knowledge, it contained a payroll for the Northwest Mounted Police, and he didn't trust these goddamn Metis, or anyone else for that matter, to be left alone with it.

Gabriel Dumont dropped down to trackside, and

glared at the winded female prostrated before him. It was some considerable time since he had enjoyed any kind of woman, and this one was undeniably special. 'When we've finished up here, you're coming with me, bitch,' he hissed, 'and who knows: if you treat me right, you might still make it to Moose Jaw. *Eventually.*'

Kirsty somehow sucked enough air into her lungs to respond. 'Go to hell, trash. I've seen better looking animals in my time!' With that, she rolled over, leapt to her feet and ran for her life away from the stationary train.

'Haw, haw,' crowed Hatcher, over by the engine. 'Seems like she's got business elsewhere.'

Dumont completely ignored him, because at that moment something happened inside his head. The rage that he felt suddenly turned deadly, over-whelming any vestige of sexual desire. He lost all interest in pursuing her. And yet if he couldn't have her, then no one else would. Drawing and cocking his Remington Revolver, he took direct aim at a spot between her shoulder blades. There was to be no warning shot, just a swift execution by way of payback. The sound of rending metal emanated from the boxcar, but it didn't even register with him.

Kirsty's only thought was to put as much distance as possible between herself and the railroad. She knew that if he chose, the half-breed could soon overtake her on horseback, but it was now obvious that his main reason for being on the train was to rob

17

it, and so hopefully he would have more pressing priorities. Running 'full chisel', her chest heaved painfully as she desperately sucked air into parched lungs. It simply never occurred to her that Dumont might actually shoot her in the back, and it was also true that she wasn't completely friendless.

'I didn't come all this way just to watch you gun down some poor defenceless woman,' Hatcher hollered over. 'Leave her be, goddamn it, and see to the passengers.'

Dumont's forefinger froze on the trigger, and then his lips twisted into a savage smile. No cursed Yankee would give him instructions. His finger contracted, and the holster gun crashed out. The .44 calibre bullet slammed into Kirsty's back, throwing her face down in the long grass. Instinctively, the Metis again cocked his weapon, but then held fire. The bitch was clearly dead, and cartridges cost money. That final thought created sudden curiosity, and so he turned towards the boxcar that was being emptied of its contents. He could sense Hatcher's angry gaze on him, but simply chose to ignore it.

Shocked faces peered through the windows of the two carriages, but no one ventured outside. The foolish young woman was obviously deceased, so there was little to be gained by inviting trouble. Besides, as the bloodied half-breed turned back towards them, they were abruptly preoccupied with safeguarding their personal possessions. It would have to be left to someone far more qualified to confront these murdering outlaws!

CHAPTER TWO

'You got no call treating us like this, Bronson,' the wounded man bleated. Blood seeped from a gunshot wound to his right shoulder, and under the hot sun he felt as though he was suffering the tortures of the damned.

Deputy United States Marshal Jesse Bronson didn't even trouble to turn in his saddle. He just bellowed back over his shoulder. 'If you don't like the treatment, don't rob the trains!'

'Hell, I weren't even there, Marshal,' another fellow protested as he massaged an aching thigh. A shotgun pellet had torn clean through the flesh, and a non-too spotless bandana had subsequently been tied tightly around it.

'You're a long-tongued liar, Sweeney,' Bronson retorted. 'I've got any number of witnesses placing you on that hold-up . . . *and* you resisted arrest.'

'That's just my contrary nature,' Sweeney whined. 'I don't mean anything by it.'

'Tell that to the judge!'

19

And so it continued as the four weary horsemen closed in on Billings, Montana from the south. Bronson was content to go along with the inconsequential banter because it passed the time. All three of his prisoners were injured, but that was usually the way of it with him. To his fashion of thinking, if you broke the law, then you forfeited any civil rights that might exist on the frontier. In fact it wasn't at all uncommon for him to bring in fugitives face down over a saddle!

Billings had come into existence as a rail hub for the Northern Pacific Railroad, and was in fact named after one of its presidents. It was situated just to the north of the Yellowstone River, and it was that watercourse which the small group was now approaching. Any joy that Bronson might have felt at the sight of fresh water was unfortunately tempered by the fact that they weren't the only riders on the move. From the direction of the city, around a dozen men were advancing steadily. They had obviously been idling in a nearby stand of trees, watching for Bronson's return, and had timed it so that they would intercept him at the river ford. It was a natural pinch point that he had no way of avoiding without getting very wet indeed, or travelling more miles than he would ever dream of just to avoid a fight.

'Well that just tears it,' the lawman muttered from under his luxurious, drooping moustache. Then, much louder, he added, 'Looks like you fellas are gonna be invited to a necktie party.'

As the wounded outlaws observed the lynch mob's

20

approach, any lingering belligerence instantly vanished. It was a fact that when they robbed trains, some of their victims usually got hurt or even killed, and sadly not everyone was content to let the law take its course. Consequently, Marshal Bronson had suddenly become their best and only hope of survival.

'You ain't thinking on handing us over to those sons of bitches . . . *are you?*' Real fear was evident in Sweeney's voice. Getting shot in a fight was one thing. Dancing on the end of a rope until hopefully your neck broke was quite another. If the brutal process was handled poorly, a man could dangle in agony for ages before finally expiring.

Bronson favoured him with a knowing smile. 'Bad deeds coming home to roost, huh?' Then his weathered features hardened. 'Well I ain't never before lost a prisoner to a mob, an' it's not going to happen now.' So saying, he single-handedly took hold of his sawn-off shotgun, settling the butt on his right thigh. The heavy iron hook, which had long since replaced his left hand, would serve to hold the reins as he slowed to a halt on the south side of the ford.

The far larger group splashed eagerly through the shallow water, until the leaders reined in a few yards from the solitary lawman. For a long moment they all waited, fingering their weapons, expecting him to open the conversation. Frustratingly, he just sat his horse, regarding them with apparent disinterest, whilst all the while waiting to see who had the words. Unsurprisingly, that turned out to be Al Meeker, who was obviously the nominal ringleader.

'One of those bastards shot and killed Pete Westby. He left a wife an' two young 'uns in Billings to fend for themselves, as well you know, Marshal.'

Bronson regarded the other man steadily. Meeker was a blustering storekeeper, who had designs on civic prominence. He also liked a drink or six, which was very probably why he was at the head of this mixed bunch of townspeople. And it was doubtless loud talk and fiery liquor that had emboldened them to tag along, but now one or two of them were already having second thoughts. All of them knew the US Marshal by sight, and many by his reputation. He took his responsibilities seriously, and was not a man to cross.

The lawman finally responded with just the one word. 'And?'

The merchant glanced at the others for support before stating his case. 'You need to step aside, and sit this one out. We're gonna hang all three from those trees over yonder. That way, whoever did it pays the price, and we get to see them hop and squeal.'

'And the two that didn't?'

Meeker shrugged. 'Who cares? They're all outlaws, ain't they?'

'Oh yeah, they're all outlawed up. I won't gainsay that. But they're also *my* prisoners, which means they'll all get their day in court.' So saying, Bronson retracted the hammers on his twelve-gauge and slowly lowered it, so that the gaping muzzles were pointing directly at the lynch mob. 'And think on this, Meeker,' he continued remorselessly, 'Stepping aside ain't my way, and assaulting a federal officer is a sure route to trouble. Even if you survive this little shindig, you'll likely end up breaking rocks in some prison. Plenty of bad things can happen to a man in such places, and so who knows, you might not even see that store of yours again. So you just go ahead and make your play, and I'll maybe forget that you're all really just decent citizens, and squeeze these triggers. A sawn-off makes a terrible mess. Either way, you've got to ask yourself, is stretching the necks of these pus weasels really worth it?'

As beads of sweat appeared on his forehead, Meeker involuntarily swallowed. With Bronson's flinty stare boring into him, he was sobering up mighty fast. Glancing around at his companions, he could see that they too were suddenly anxious to be elsewhere. 'Yeah, well,' he finally managed. 'I guess we might could have been a bit hasty, Marshal.' The acknowledgment was given reluctantly, but was clearly supported by everyone in the now defunct lynch mob.

The lawman nodded, but his demeanour softened not a jot. 'So get out of the damn way, all of you! I've got ten days of trail dust to wash off.' So saying, he urged his mount forward, compelling the good citizens of Billings to pull clear rapidly. Knowing full well that his prisoners would be even more eager to quit the place, he didn't trouble to check behind him. Instead, he waited until he was level with the chastened storekeeper, before abruptly allowing his body to drop down low to the left. The iron hook that had replaced his fingers looped around the front of Meeker's left ankle, and then he pulled upwards with great force.

With a cry of dismay, the helpless storekeeper toppled from his horse and down into the Yellowstone River. Soaking and shaken, he lay in the water and gazed up at his assailant reproachfully.

'Hot dang, if that don't beat all,' Sweeney announced gleefully.

Bronson favoured his victim with a chill glance. 'Drunk or sober, it makes no matter. Just you be sure to step wide of me from now on, Al Meeker!' With that, he spurred his animal forward and rode off without a backward glance.

'You must be getting soft in your old age, Jesse,' observed United States Marshal Robert Kelley. 'You've actually brought all three prisoners in alive.'

Bronson chuckled. 'Yeah, but the sawbones hasn't finished with them yet, and he loses more than he saves.'

The two men were sitting companionably in Kelley's office in the federal courthouse building, sipping from mugs filled with what passed for coffee. The door was wide open to allow some much-needed throughput of air. The summer had barely arrived, but already it was shaping up to be a hot one.

At fifty-five years of age, Kelley boasted a heavy beard and full moustache, and as usual appeared to have something on his mind. Which was not surpris-ing, really, considering the vast amount of unsettled

24

territory that he was responsible for policing. And then there was always the unexpected, which could just come out of nowhere, courtesy of the goddamn telegraph network.

'Come on, Bob, out with it,' his long-serving deputy demanded. 'I can always tell when you're chewing something over.'

The marshal peered at him pensively and grunted. 'OK, OK. There's no painless way to say this, so I'll just up and come out with it. I realize that you only just rode back in yesterday afternoon, *and* that you didn't have an easy time of it, but I have got another assignment for you. An' this one's definitely a bit different, because it'll mean you heading north of the line.'

Bronson was genuinely puzzled. 'Line? What line?'

Kelley sighed impatiently. 'The border into Canada.'

The other man was dumbfounded. 'The hell you say! And just what is there up north that concerns us?'

The marshal stood up and began pacing his office. 'Two particular hardcases, citizens of these United States, have seen fit to start robbing trains in the Province of Saskatchewan. And don't ask me to try and spell that, because I can't! Anyhu, you might know of them. One is Brin Carson, and the other Vern Hatcher, also sometimes known as Thatcher.'

Bronson grimaced. 'Oh, I know what he's sometimes known as, the son of a bitch! He's definitely unfinished business for the marshals . . . In fact they

25

both are. And for my money, Carson will be the brains behind anything that's happening up there. He's one dangerous *hombre*.'

Kelley nodded. 'Well it seems like the Canadians aren't used to handling our train robbers and road agents, because the government in Ottawa has asked for some assistance in hunting them down. And, in an amazing spirit of cooperation, Washington has actually agreed. And then, out of the kindness of his heart, the Attorney General promptly turned the problem over to me, being as Montana is the nearest US Territory.'

Bronson scratched his bristly chin. He knew he would probably regret asking his next question. 'So why me in particular?'

There was a momentary pause as Kelley struggled to control his expression. 'Because you've worked with a certain Mountie before, and by all accounts you got on famously.'

'Oh shit!'

CHAPTER THREE

Jesse Bronson heaved his saddle and long guns down off the open platform of the Canadian Pacific Railroad carriage and took his first look at the town of Moose Jaw. With Saskatchewan's seemingly limitless southern plains pretty much devoid of trees, the buildings were either constructed of prairie sod or rough-cut timber, the latter freighted west at great expense on the new railroad. In truth, it wasn't much different from so many other frontier settlements that he had visited over the years, except that it was located at a far higher latitude, which meant that life sure would be mighty hard come winter!

With easy access to water always a prime requirement, the town had developed near the confluence of Moose Jaw River and Thunder Creek. In the past, Assiniboine and Cree Indians had camped there, as had Metis buffalo hunters when there had still been such creatures to slaughter. Now, the 'big shaggies' had all gone, replaced by cattle ranching, and Moose Jaw was beholden to the railroad for its prosperity.

Unfortunately, there were those who would prey on the 'Iron Horse', and so they too would need to be hunted down.

As Bronson stepped clear of the track, he suddenly spotted a tall, bearded figure striding towards him. Samuel Bairstow was resplendent in the distinctive scarlet Norfolk jacket of a Northwest Mounted Policeman, around which sat a brown leather gun-belt supporting a military style flap holster. Below this, he wore steel grey coloured cord breeches that had obviously seen a lot of use. All in all, he made quite an impressive sight. And something had changed since their time together in Montana.

'Hey, you've gone and got yourself another stripe, *Sergeant*,' the marshal called out, as the 'Queen's Cowboy' drew nearer.

The amiable handshake that they shared contrasted sharply with their original chill meeting in Kelley's office some eighteen months earlier. Then, Bronson had been characteristically antagonistic towards an unwanted partner, but gradually, over the course of time, mutual respect culminating in genuine regard had grown between them. Another thing had changed as well: in the United States, it was Bairstow who had had to rely on others for local knowledge, but now it was the American who was a stranger in a strange land.

The Mountie's smile was genuinely warm, and tellingly it reached his eyes, but it didn't last for long. As his handsome features slipped into repose, anxiety was plain to see. Here was obviously a man

28

with troubles on his mind, but for a brief period whatever they were could wait. 'It seems like an awful long time since Great Falls, Montana,' he remarked. 'How's about I buy you a steak, and maybe even a drink, Marshal?'

That man rubbed his belly in sudden anticipation. 'I thought you were never gonna ask.'

Hopkins' Dining Parlour was a pretty fancy name for a rough-cut timber building with creaky chairs, but Bronson couldn't have asked for better food, and Bairstow was considerate enough to let him eat his fill before talking business. During the meal they casually reminisced of times past, and it became obvious that the Mountie's appetite was not what it had been. It was only as they sipped genuine hot coffee, liberally laced with whiskey, that the American began with what seemed to be an obvious question.

'So whose money did they steal?'

'Government money,' was the rather terse response.

Bronson peered at him quizzically. There was more to this. 'For what use was it intended . . . *exactly?*'

Bairstow sighed. 'If you must know, it was the Mounted Police payroll. Cash money to pay all the force in the Northwest Territories on its way to head-quarters at Fort Walsh. For what it's worth, that's some way west of here. More's the pity.'

The marshal just couldn't restrain his mirth. 'Haw,

haw, haw. No wonder you're looking sick. You haven't been paid.'

His companion grinned ruefully, but the good cheer was fleeting. The red-coated Mountie was still a big strapping fellow, but something about him had definitely changed. There was sadness to his demeanour that hadn't existed during their earlier time together. And Bronson wasn't one to beat about the bush.

'Just what is it that ails you, Samuel? Something sure as hell does.'

Bairstow jerked slightly with surprise, before raising a sad smile. 'My wife is like to die, Jesse.'

'Your wife?'

'Yeah. I married Kirsty. Kirsty Landers as was. And one of those bastard train robbers shot her in the back and left her for dead. She wasn't even armed, for Christ sake!'

Bronson's eyes narrowed. 'Yankee or Metis?'

'Seems like he was one of ours. Your fellas contented themselves with merely killing the fireman.'

'So how do you want to play this?'

Baistow's eyebrows rose. 'You're asking me?'

The marshal smiled. 'This is your country, remember? I'm the visitor this time. Hell, I don't even have jurisdiction up here.'

Rather than tease him over that fact, the Mountie merely grunted. 'Well, first off, I'll take you to see Kirsty. But don't expect conversation . . . of any kind. She hasn't uttered a single goddamn word since being brought home.'

*

Kirsty Bairstow lay on one side of the double bed in the large sod cabin that served as both home and office for her husband. Her normally healthy complexion had a waxy sheen, and her breath came in shallow draughts. Heavy bandaging encased her upper body. There was no recognition of the visitor, because her eyelids remained closed, just twitching occasionally as though triggered by bad memories.

'She's been like this since the doc extracted the bullet,' the Mountie explained despondently, tears welling up in his eyes. 'I tell you, Jesse, if she dies, I don't know what I'll do.'

Bronson, who had never got around to marrying anyone, and whose only female companions were Montana whores, nevertheless nodded understandingly. He had remembered Kirsty as a dynamic and extremely attractive girl. Hardened to the results of violence as he was, the sight of her there shocked him. Yet unfortunately, there was absolutely nothing he could do to help her, so it made sense to stick with what he was good at.

'Best not to think on it, Samuel,' he replied softly. 'It won't do you no good. What we *can* do is set about finding the bull turds that did this. Thing is, are you right sure you want to go off and leave her alone in this condition?'

The other man nodded soberly. 'There ain't nothing more I can do for Kirsty here, and there's a widow woman from the town who I can trust to watch

31

NORTH OF THE LINE

over her. Problem is,' he admitted reluctantly, 'I ain't too sure where to start with all this. Train robbery is a bit different to cattle rustling and such.'

Bronson had been giving the matter a deal of thought on his long journey. 'These fellas could be hiding out anywhere. Thing is, who knew about the money on that train?'

That got Bairstow thinking, and as he did so the anxiety that he felt for Kirsty faded slightly from his features. Leading the marshal outside, as though instinctively concerned that their talk might disturb her, he began to put two and two together. 'Regina has got the biggest Canadian Pacific depot in the province, as you'll have seen on your way here. Someone there had to have known about it.'

Bronson nodded encouragingly. 'Carson and Hatcher are old hands at this. Their gang carried out a few raids on westbound trains in Nebraska. They bought or bullied some Union Pacific employee in Omaha into giving them information on train shipments. That too has a big railroad depot. They made a tidy penny until it all got too hot for them, which is very likely why they came up here. There were no loose ends either. The probable informant was found in an alley with his throat cut from ear to ear.' He paused momentarily, as something else occurred to him. 'And has the payroll been replaced yet?'

The Mountie stared at him wide-eyed. 'No. It hasn't. I suppose it'll take a while to organize so much cash again. Christ, you don't think they'd try exactly the same thing again, do you?'

'It's what I'd do! More to the point, it's exactly what they've done before. I know, because I've checked.'

Bairstow was hooked. Suddenly he had no thought for anything else. 'And I suppose you're going to tell me how we tackle them.'

Bronson favoured him with a lopsided grin. 'Well, that's what I came all this way for. Only thing is, what I propose comes with a shitload of risk. Whoever you answer to might see it as a big ask.'

'Just tell me,' the Mountie insisted.

'Where did this Dumont cuss board the train?'

'Regina.'

The marshal nodded, as though everything was so clear. 'So for my money, that's where it all hinges. When the next payroll heads west, you make damn sure the depot knows all about it. And this time, when the train comes through Regina, you an' me will already be locked in the boxcar with all that lovely cash. But no visible guards, else wise it'll frighten them off, for sure.'

Bairstow frowned. 'We'll almost certainly be heavily outnumbered. It's one heck of a risk.'

'Ain't it just?'

The Canadian regarded him pensively for long moments before finally coming to a decision. 'What the hell, why not? But we'll have to go to Regina and get permission from my inspector. It's too important to chance using the telegraph ... and besides,' he added archly, 'he hasn't had the pleasure of meeting you yet!'

Bronson stared at him blankly. 'Inspector! What's he do, punch tickets?'

Despite everything troubling him, Bairstow chuckled. 'You've got a lot to learn about the Mounted Police, Jesse Bronson. Inspector Longshanks is my superior officer.'

The American shook his head with disbelief. '*Longshanks*! What the hell kind of a name is that?'

'An *English* name, my Yankee friend; in case you'd forgotten, you're not in Montana anymore.'

And so it was decided. The next eastbound train to Regina would have the two very different lawmen on board. As once before, their mutual fate was now closely entwined.

Inspector Simon Longshanks of the Northwest Mounted Police stared incredulously at the two men standing before him. Having listening very carefully to the sergeant's scheme, the colour in his face was rapidly approaching that of their scarlet jackets. The inspector was a heavyset whiskered man of middle years, whose gold braid clearly emphasised the gulf between his commissioned rank and that of his subordinate. The formality of the situation was a world away from anything Jesse Bronson had previously experienced.

'You realize what you're asking, don't you?' Longshanks almost shouted. 'I appreciate that you have a personal interest in all of this, which no doubt exceeds your sworn duty to the police service. I am deeply saddened by the condition of your wife, but after the loss of thousands of Canadian dollars to those accursed blackguards, you want me to advertise the arrival of a replacement shipment, *and then* allow the two of you alone to guard it. Do you think I'm a blithering idiot?'

It was possibly unfortunate that Bronson considered that to be an open question. 'It's too early to tell, mister,' he retorted. 'I've only just visited with you.'

The strained interview was now beginning to take on the doomed appearance of a transatlantic coffin ship. But with a horrified Bairstow standing rigidly to attention, and his equally formal superior momentarily lost for words, the deputy marshal just ploughed on regardless. 'I don't know about this Dumont cuss, but Carson and Hatcher sure ain't got any kind of death wish that I know of. And they're with folks that know the country, and ain't set to be humbugged. If you fill the boxcar and carriages with armed men, they're bound to find out somehow. The payroll will be safe for sure. *But* you'll never catch those murdering road agents, will you? Yet if you just sneak the two of us onto the train, on the quiet, with a sawn-off apiece and plenty of shells . . . well, we could net you quite a haul. And that's the which of why I'm here . . . ain't it?'

For a seemingly endless moment there was stunned silence. Bairstow kept his eyes firmly in the middle distance. Longshanks opened his mouth to speak, before abruptly closing it again. Then, sitting behind his desk in the timber framed office, he digested the American's words thoroughly before finally coming to a decision. Only then did he respond, with his impressive mutton-chop whiskers again appearing to move with a life of their own.

'You're the first United States lawman that I've had the *pleasure* of encountering, Marshal Bronson. And whilst I freely admit to not understanding some of your colourful patois, I *can* see the sense in what you said. And apparently you were sent up here at our request, so it would be churlish of me to ignore your advice. I will put *your* suggestion to the superintendent. For something of this magnitude, it will have to be his decision, and I will certainly not be mentioning the use of sawn-off shotguns. That will be a little too American for his tastes. We don't have the gun law of your frontier, and we most definitely don't want it!'

Bronson's eyes narrowed. He had been considering querying the meaning of 'magnitude', but that last comment had really taken the cake. 'Well, whether you like it or not, *Inspector*, trouble has come at you across the border, and you might could need all the help you can get to handle it. Especially as you seem to have plenty of home-grown felons of your own!' With that, he flipped a casual salute and left the office without a backward glance.

Longshanks glanced at his subordinate in disbelief. 'Is he always like that?'

Bairstow had to focus on controlling his expression. 'Pretty much.' And then he remembered whom he was addressing. 'Sir.'

Josiah Applegate touched the lower right side of his mouth very gingerly. For days he had been suffering agonies from a tooth. Then a reluctant trip to the sawbones resulted in an offer of extraction or the opportunity to try oil of cloves. Since the first option, likely administered without anaesthetic, would undoubtedly be excruciatingly painful, he had decided to try the latter. And amazingly it was giving him a noticeable measure of relief. Then he saw two very disparate figures approaching his booth, and the awful throbbing returned with a vengeance.

Applegate worked in the Canadian Pacific's ticket office in Regina, and he nursed a very guilty secret. Privy to all the railroad's news and gossip, and hopelessly addicted to gambling, he had fallen in with extremely bad company, some of which was about to pay him a visit.

Dumont and Carson had waited patiently until their prey was alone, and now carefully scrutinised their surroundings before moving around to the side door. With great reluctance the clerk moved to unlock it, and only then because he knew that if obstructed they would likely kick it in.

'You must be mad,' he hissed as the two men crowded in. 'What if someone recognizes you from the hold-up?'

Dumont regarded him scornfully. 'People are like so many chickens. They were too busy shitting themselves to stare at us.'

'Besides, they were all travelling away from here,' the American added with somewhat greater logic. Then he sniffed the air around Applegate suspiciously. 'What the hell's that stink?' he demanded.

The clerk coloured with embarrassment, and instinctively shifted the cotton pad in his mouth. 'Clove oil,' he mumbled. 'I've got a tooth that's giving me fits, and it's provided a measure of relief.'

'Jesus,' Carson exclaimed. 'I'd rather let a blacksmith rive it out. Even a ten-dollar whore is gonna keep well clear of you with that in, and she'd give you way more relief!'

'Enough of this shit,' Dumont snarled. Habitually reeking of body odour and animal grease, he appeared oblivious to the smell. Abruptly getting uncomfortably close, the Metis slapped Applegate's jaw vindictively at its most tender spot. As the other man's eyes filled with tears, he continued, 'You know exactly why we're here. What have you got for us?'

Fear took over from pain, and the clerk glanced furtively around. 'If I tell you, I'll likely lose my job for sure. The Mounties are all fired up over what you did, an' it's not just about the money. That woman you shot only happened to be married to one of them,' he added accusingly. 'If they connect me to that, they'll lock me up and throw away the key!'

None of that meant anything to Carson. His sharp mind had seized on the first sentence. The snivelling turd definitely had something to impart. 'It's us you need to be afeared of, not the goddamn Mounties.

They're just peacocks, strutting around in fancy uniforms. And you got well paid last time, didn't you? So out with it, what do you know?' A momentary pause, and then, 'Or it'll go badly for you!'

Applegate's eyes widened like saucers. Although there wasn't really a great deal in it, it was possibly the Metis who frightened him most. There was an animal-like quality to the half-breed, and the clerk had heard terrible tales of their penchant for using skinning knives on victims. It was also a fact that after the first robbery he *had* got well paid in shiny dollars. Unfortunately he had lost most of it at the tables, and was actually in debt to one of the more unforgiving gambling halls. That, and the prospect of a honed blade in his vitals, brought about a change of heart. And, as Carson had surmised, he *did* have news for them.

'Very well,' he began reluctantly. 'They're sending more money out from the east . . . by train, of course. And here's the thing,' he continued, excitement growing despite his fear. 'It won't be guarded!'

That was greeted with disbelief by the American. 'What about your tarnal redcoats? They might be peacocks, but I'll wager they still carry guns. And at the very least they're gonna have a score to settle with my trigger-happy *amigo* here.'

Dumont scowled at his crony, but chose to remain silent. He wanted to listen to Applegate's response, and that man didn't disappoint. Growing in confidence, he tapped the side of his nose. 'From what I hear, there's an Indian scare in Alberta. Seems like some folks might just be selling liquor to the tribes. Ain't it terrible what some people will do for money?' The clerk sniggered at his own attempt at levity, but realizing that no one else had joined in, hurriedly continued. 'Anyway, the Blackfoot are causing trouble south of Calgary, and most of the Mounties have been sent west. *And* nobody believes you'd be fool enough to try the exact same thing again. They think you're probably long gone.' With that, he stopped and watched the outlaws guardedly.

For seemingly an age, the two men regarded each other pensively. Then, finally, Brin Carson broke into a smile. 'What the hell . . . If I'm gonna end up a corpse, I might as well be a rich one, and your story *has* got a ring of truth to it. Seems like you've done good, railroad man.' He reached out to playfully pat the clerk's cheek, causing that individual to flinch and back off.

And yet, even under stress, some instincts never weaken. 'Good enough to get some cash on account?' Applegate queried eagerly.

In the blink of an eye, a knifepoint appeared under his chin. 'When *we* get paid, little man, then *you* get paid,' Dumont rasped dangerously. 'Unless you want me to remove that tooth on account. I'd enjoy watching you cry like a baby!'

CHAPTER FOUR

'It's just a pure shame we couldn't bring any horses,' Bronson commented sadly. 'We might have need to chase down those sons of bitches, if'n they don't all get paroled to Jesus or surrender.'

Samuel Bairstow shrugged. 'The two of us sneaking on board in the dead of night was one thing, hiding a couple of animals in here entirely another.'

The two lawmen were lounging on the floor of the shaking, rattling boxcar. The only light was that which came through the chinks in the timber walls, but it was enough for their purposes. Behind them, with more padlocks than they could shake a stick at, was a substantial reinforced strongbox containing the replacement payroll. They had joined the train at the town of Indian Head, some forty or so miles east of Regina. That way, if any outlaws posing as passengers got on at the latter, they wouldn't spot anything untoward.

'Is that inspector of yours for real?' the marshal queried. 'He's like a stuffed shirt. I ain't never seen

41

the like before, not even in the military.'

The Mountie chuckled. 'He's not so bad, really. He means well, and he has a lot of responsibilities. He's not just a law officer, he's also a Justice of the Peace.'

That meant nothing special to the American. 'A peace officer's no different to me.'

Bairstow suddenly gazed at him with a noticeable air of superiority. 'When you arrest a felon, all supposing you don't kill him first, can you try *and* sentence him as well? Because Longshanks and others like him can.'

'Hot dang!' the other man responded. 'You mean he's judge, jury and executioner, all rolled up into one?'

'A bit like that,' the Canadian allowed.

'Shit in a bucket! That's a job to die for! I might just have to move up here permanently!'

With both towns now behind them and the sun well and truly up, Bronson was getting restless. Their rather stodgy diet included copious quantities of beans, and locked in the boxcar as they were, the inevitable by-product meant that the air was getting decidedly potent.

'Goddamn it, it'll be worth being attacked just to get some fresh air in here,' he exclaimed.

The words were hardly out of his mouth when the brakes were slammed on with such urgency that if the lawmen hadn't already been on the floor they would certainly have ended up on it. Even locked away at the rear of the train, the shrill squealing was clearly audible.

'Since that can't be buffalo on the tracks anymore, it looks like you've got your wish,' Bairstow retorted croakily, his face suddenly grim. Brutal, bloody violence was an unfortunate part of their job, and he should have been used to it by then, but his mouth never failed to go dry at the prospect.

The marshal smiled encouragingly. He was older and far more hardened to the nastier aspects of law enforcement. He also possessed an instinctive understanding of positioning. And so, peering around the interior, Bronson knew immediately where he needed to be. As the train slowed to a halt, he crawled over to the far corner, furthest away from the single sliding door, and lay down. As ever, the safest place to be was on the floor, and in this instance well clear of the strongbox.

'Pick your spot,' he hissed at the Mountie.

That man seemed to come to his senses, and clambered over quickly to the opposite corner, in line with the sliding door. Then, almost simultaneously, there were four audible clicks as the lawmen retracted the hammers on their shotguns. The muzzles of Bairstow's still bore the marks of the saw that had been used to shorten the weapon hastily. Longshanks hadn't been jesting. Sawn-off shotguns were definitely not part of the Mounties' armoury. Both men also drew their revolvers, and placed them on the floor in easy reach. The holster-guns reflected their differing nationalities. Bronson carried a ruggedly reliable Remington, whilst his companion possessed the Adams, quintessentially British and known for its stopping power.

The marshal peered through the dust raised by the sudden braking and winked, before indicating that he would make the first move. For better or for worse they were ready. Whatever happened next would likely be at least partially out of their control, but one thing was for sure . . . there was going to be some dying!

Everything had gone so smoothly, which perversely meant that Brin Carson was unaccountably on edge. The westbound train had arrived on time, with no visible guards, and had come to an enforced halt in almost the same place as before. That little shit Applegate had apparently come good, yet the hardened outlaw rarely accepted anything at face value. And so, as the Metis saboteurs eagerly raced for the boxcar, he suddenly bellowed for them to stop. Dumont glared at the American impatiently, but possessed the sense not to countermand him. He was slowly discovering that the Yankees were not just full of piss and vinegar alone.

Carson glanced over at Hatcher, who had the engine's crew under his gun. Thankfully, that man hadn't yet shot either of them. 'How's about bringing those grease monkeys over here? They can be first in the boxcar.'

Slow on the uptake, his partner shrugged, but didn't object. Gesturing with his revolver, he ordered the engineer and fireman out of the cab. Those men well knew what had happened during the last hold-up. Nervous and sweating profusely, they dropped to the ground reluctantly and walked towards the rear of what *had* been their train. As they passed the two passenger carriages, they were aware of numerous frightened faces peering out at them.

'Just what are you aiming to do with us, mister?' the engineer demanded of Carson.

That individual smiled darkly. 'Only right you should get a look-see at your own cargo. Step on up to this door, the pair of you.'

Only when they had done so did he nod at Dumont. 'Open her up, why don't you? *But* these two get to go in first. Savvy?'

The half-breed wasn't stupid. And along with understanding came a sly smile on his brutalised features. A few blows with a hammer smashed off the padlock, and eager hands reached for the sliding door.

'In you get, fellas,' Carson ordered, prodding one of them with the muzzle of his revolver. 'Be sure to tell us what you find!'

Samuel Bairstow's heart jumped as the big door slid back noisily. It slammed to a stop mere inches from his head, allowing bright sunlight to flood in, but also effectively blocking any view of the outside. As Bronson had anticipated, it would be left to him to call the shots . . . quite literally.

The two lawmen were sadly oblivious to the

appalling turn of events. They had heard some shouting, but what with their own incarceration and the noise of the steam engine, it had all sounded garbled. Only now was there any chance of clarity, but their immediate surroundings had fallen strangely quiet. Then a hand appeared, followed by scuffling sounds as a bulky figure slowly heaved himself aboard. Bronson's forefinger tightened on a trigger as he shifted the twelve-gauge over to cover the intruder.

It was the quantity of grime on the man's face that undoubtedly saved his life. He clearly belonged on a footplate, rather than in a jail. Grubby overalls only served to confirm that supposition. Bronson held fire, but as the engineer looked to his right and spotted the gaping muzzles, he froze in horror. Then there was a rush of liquid, and an expanding pool appeared at his feet.

'Oh Jesus, mister,' he pleaded. 'Don't shoot me, for pity's sake!'

The marshal's only response was a gentle sigh. Things definitely weren't panning out as he'd expected, which served as a reminder that he wasn't just up against run of the mill outlaws. Then a vaguely familiar voice called out. 'Who all's in there? Speak up, or I'll blow a hole in his back!'

Bronson already knew whom he was pursuing, but hearing that still made him curse under his breath. Brin Carson had apparently got the jump on him, and it rankled. It rankled a lot! Glancing to his left, he gestured to Bairstow that he should reply, and just prayed that the Mountie had his wits about him. He soon found out.

'This is Sergeant Samuel Bairstow of the Northwest Mounted Police. Drop your weapons. You're all under arrest. If you harm this man, it will be all the worse for you.'

Beyond the wooden walls, there was a stunned silence as the gang members looked askance at each other. Dumont in particular, impressed by his fore-thought, stared at Carson with something approaching respect. It was Vern Hatcher who finally responded, and in fairly typical fashion.

'Haw, haw haw. Just how do you propose to arrest us when you can't even see us?'

To his credit, Bairstow was ready for that one, and happy to sow some uncertainty amongst the robbers. 'We knew all about your pathetic little plans for this train, which must make you wonder who you can trust. And there'll be a party of Mounties boiling across that plain in a matter of minutes. If you're still holding your firearms, they'll shoot any man on sight.'

As expected, there was another silence as the train robbers scanned the surrounding horizon. With absolutely nothing in sight, fear soon turned to dis-belief. On the open prairie, it would be nigh on impossible for any number of horsemen to approach unseen at speed. Again it was Hatcher who had the words.

'Too thin, law dog. Too thin! I've heard all about you redcoats. Most of you are off chasing Injuns . . .

or leastways their squaws. Which means you're out here on your lonesome, trying to make a name for yourself. But we ain't under your gun, see? So you got nothing.' He turned to the others and chuckled, but he was given little time to enjoy his eloquence.

'What we *have* got is the money, Vern Hatcher,' Bronson abruptly barked out.

'Shit in a bucket!' Carson exclaimed. 'I know that voice. Is that you, Bronson? You old bastard.'

'The very same, Brin Carson. Now do as my partner here said, and drop your weapons.'

The marshal's name meant nothing to the Metis, but the two Americans shook their heads in disbelief. He was the last person they had expected to encounter north of the 49th Parallel, and it set them to thinking mighty hard. What if there were more federal officers on the train? Consequently, it was Gabriel Dumont who abruptly took over the negotiations.

'I don't care who you are in there. We got prisoners. So if you don't hand the cash money over, we kill them all, one by one.' He paused to emit a chuckle. 'You ain't so smart now, eh?'

Inside the boxcar, the two lawmen stared intently at each other as though desperately seeking a solution in the others eyes. It was Bronson who quietly put their dilemma into words. 'They ain't bluffing. We stonewall them, and innocent folks'll get to dying.'

A quick glance at the terrified engineer only served to confirm the dire plight. His staring eyes were pleading frantically with them to agree on any terms. Colour began to drain from Bairstow's face as he reached the only possible decision. He well knew who would get the blame for all this, because the marshal was just a visitor . . . even if it had been all his idea. With great reluctance, he nodded and whispered, 'Give them the goddamn money.'

Bronson understood all too well the likely cost of such a choice, and not just the fact that the Mountie now still wouldn't get paid. 'OK, it's yours,' he called out in genuine disgust. 'But we ain't bringing it to you.'

Malicious glee spread over Dumont's features as he glanced around at his cronies. He gestured for some of his Metis followers to move nearer the boxcar, and then called back, 'So let the railroad man bring it out.'

Bronson sighed with resignation. 'Yeah, yeah,' was all he could think to reply. Then to the engineer he instructed quietly, 'Do as he said. Once it's out there, try and back off away from them. *If* you get chance.'

Realizing he wasn't safe yet, that man nodded vigorously and then moved over to the strongbox. Desperate to be out of the limelight, he didn't even attempt to pick it up, but instead grabbed the handle at one end and dragged it rapidly over to the doorway. He then dropped down to trackside with a great sigh of relief. Whatever else happened, at least he no longer had two shotguns aimed at him. However, he wasn't out of it yet.

Carson had little trust in any man, and certainly

not lawmen, so his orders were brusque. 'Get that box over here, away from the train, and then stick around. You're a hostage, remember?'

As the engineer complied, Dumont directed four of his men to keep the boxcar covered and the other two to watch the passengers. He would have the pleasure of smashing open the strongbox. And yet it soon became apparent that such a task was not a matter of moments. Even swinging a heavy crowbar vigorously, the half-breed could make no impression on it. Reinforced with steel bars, and multiple padlocks, the box had been deliberately constructed to require concerted effort. And that would take time!

Vern Hatcher, never known for his patience, was getting restless. 'Enough of this shit; let's just blast it,' he snarled, aiming his revolver at one of the locks.

'Belay that,' came Carson's surprisingly nautical command. 'We start shooting, an' those law dogs might just get to thinking we've killed the crew, and so decide they've nothing to lose by taking us on.'

'Well we've got to do *something*,' his partner retorted.

'Torch the boxcar,' Dumont snarled. 'Burn those damned lawmen to death. Then we can do as we please.'

Carson's response was scathing. 'Don't be a tarnal fool. Killing both a US Marshal and a Mountie just for the hell of it would be a sure way to a noose. And who's to say there *aren't* more of them out there somewhere,' he added, gesturing vaguely at the vast prairie around them.

'Who you calling a fool, Yankee dog?' the Metis leader retorted, his voice suddenly low and dangerous. Sensing trouble, his men began to turn away from the train so as to watch the unloved Americans for any signs of aggression.

Inside the boxcar, Bronson decided that the time had come to start taking chances. Unbeknown to the raiders, although there was only one way into the boxcar, there were actually two ways out. Under his prone body was a trapdoor allowing egress onto the track, and it was high time to utilize it.

'Watch the doorway,' he hissed and then rolled to one side. With his only hand, he heaved on an iron ring attached to the timber, raising the door on its hinges. Below him, on the side furthest away from the outlaws, a single rail was visible attached to a crosstie on the packed track ballast. Lowering himself carefully through the narrow opening, so as to obtain a firm footing either side of the rail, he whispered, 'Wait 'til I make my move. Savvy?'

Bairstow gave him a thumbs up, and then the marshal dropped down onto his haunches below the boxcar. The barrels of the shotgun were held steady in his iron hook as he peered through the gaps between the wheels. The view that this afforded meant that only legs of various shapes and sizes could be seen stationed along the trackside and near the strongbox. Two sets helpfully wore overalls, which marked them out as the railroad employees. Yet their presence also made things mighty awkward for his sawn-off's wide spread of shot. Time, however, was

51

running out rapidly.

'We can't stand around here mouthing off at each other,' Vern Hatcher protested, before echoing his partner's fear. 'This is a train robbery, for Christ's sake, and there might yet be a posse out there some-place.'

'Damn right,' Carson affirmed, his arms spread wide in a conciliatory fashion. 'Let's just forget the lawmen, tote that box away from here and break into it later. What do you say, Gabriel? Huh?'

That Metis grunted something unintelligible, but he must have been somewhat mollified, because he instructed two of his followers to fetch the horses. Unless Bronson made a move immedi-ately, the whole gang would be gone and out of reach of the stranded lawmen. Remaining con-cealed, he shifted slightly to the left. Sadly, the ringleaders were still too close to the train's crew, so he would have to strike at the minions. Taking a deep breath, he muttered, 'Here goes nothing,' and squeezed a trigger.

A charge of lead shot scythed into the knees of his first victim. As that man crumpled to the ground wailing in agony, Bronson, his ears ringing from the blast, altered his aim slightly and fired again. The gang members must have been on a hair trigger, because even as Bronson scrambled to a new posi-tion, he knew that his second shot hadn't been so effective. A few pieces of lead had caught one of the half-breeds whilst on the move, drawing blood, but not crippling him.

'He's under the car,' Dumont yelled. 'Shoot the bastard!'

Gunshots duly rang out, sending hot lead ricocheting off the wheels and metalwork around the spot where Bronson had been seconds earlier. Reloading his shotgun, the marshal knew that unless he maintained the pressure, the next shots would likely be aimed at one of the crew. It was at that instant that Samuel Bairstow, taking advantage of the mayhem, unleashed his own shotgun from the doorway of the boxcar. With the benefit of height and close range, his first attempt simply couldn't miss. The full blast struck a Metis in the chest, tearing a bloody hole in it, and killing him instantly.

Before he could try again, the Mountie had to duck back undercover to avoid a hasty return fire. Making best use of the time, he replaced the single empty cartridge and waited for Bronson to again draw their fire. He recognized that, with the outlaws out in the open and under deadly threat, the tables had turned abruptly. And he wasn't the only one to realize the fact.

'Forget the law dogs. We've got what we came for,' Carson bellowed. 'Let's ride!' So saying, he grabbed one side of the strongbox and waited for his buddy to do the same.

Dumont was suddenly torn by conflicting emotions. One of his men was dead for sure, but another lay on the ground, bleeding profusely and quite likely crippled. There was a creed amongst the closely-knit Metis that one man should always watch

53

out for another. Yet at the same time, the cash box was about to depart with the damned Yankees! And this wouldn't be the first occasion in Dumont's brutal existence when greed had taken precedence, although he knew that he would later genuinely regret what he was about to do. So, after firing another shot at the boxcar he yelled at them, 'We stay together, *mes amis, oui?*'

Still crouched under the boxcar, Bronson understood what was happening. Quickly backing out onto the far side of the track, he set off running towards the front of the train. That way he remained under cover whilst closing on the horses. It was obvious that most of the outlaws would get away, but if he could seize a minimum of two animals, then at least some form of pursuit would be possible. It was as he ran past the front carriage that he encountered the engineer and fireman. They had sensibly bolted at the first sign of disarray amongst the outlaws. Temporarily ignoring them, the marshal kept on going, his breathing growing increasingly ragged. He really wasn't used to this running shit.

No longer under fire, Bairstow peered out through the doorway and saw only fleeing men as his erstwhile assailants made for their horses. It was extreme range for a sawn-off but, 'What the hell,' he decided. Gripping the forestock firmly, he squeezed both triggers at once. As the big gun bucked in his grip, a cloud of powder smoke momentarily obscured his view, but the howls of pain said it all. At least some of the lead shot had found flesh and blood.

'Be sure an' take *all* the horses,' Carson bellowed as they approached the ground-tethered animals. He and Hatcher were carrying the strongbox between them, and had so far escaped any injury.

'I'll do the telling!' Dumont snarled: his hot temper had been inflamed by the blood trickling from a fresh gouge in his neck.

The seven survivors of the hold-up made for their own mounts, and yanked the picket pins out of the ground swiftly. Despite, or maybe because of Carson's order, two of them remained secured. And, struggling to both mount up and retain the strong-box, neither of the Americans were able to let loose the spare animals. Dumont briefly considered doing so, but then the urgency to be off was compounded by Bronson's sudden appearance at the front of the engine. As the now mounted outlaws streamed off across the plains, that man again discharged his shotgun to speed them on their way.

'One for the road, you bastards,' he muttered, knowing full well that in reality his task had only just begun.

CHAPTER FIVE

Sadly, the outlaws' hasty departure brought no respite, only a new set of priorities.

'Get the passengers working on the track, pronto,' Bronson instructed the crew. 'When you get to the next town, tell the folks there what occurred, and that we are in hot pursuit. Savvy?'

The engineer nodded eagerly. 'And thanks, mister.'

'For what?'

'Not blowing my head off with that scatter-gun.'

The marshal merely grunted. He had far more important matters on his mind. First off, there were two nervous horses still ground-tethered, and he wanted them. Glancing speculatively over at the crippled Metis, he saw Bairstow bearing down on him, and so dismissed them from his mind. After slinging the shotgun over his shoulder, he wedged the crown of his hat within the iron hook, thereby leaving his only hand free. Then, approaching the animals with his left arm extended, he fooled them into believing that the hat held some treat or other, and so was able to seize their reins. So far, so good.

The Mountie still had his shotgun cocked and ready. The Metis might be down and hurting, but he had a six-gun within reach. Even when that was safely tucked in his belt, tension still charged his powerful frame. There were certain questions that he needed answers to, and he would accept no refusal.

'Which one of you pus weasels shot my wife?'

The train robber gazed up at him with anguished eyes. Blood seeped from numerous deep cuts on and around his knees. Clearly in agony, he just managed, 'Wife. What wife?'

'The young woman on the train that you robbed,' Bairstow rapped out.

Despite his pain, the half-breed chose an unfortunate and foolish response. 'Oh, her. She was yours, huh? You chose well. She was a pretty one. But you can go to hell, redcoat!'

'You'll be there first if you don't tell me.'

The only reply was a stream of phlegm on the lawman's boots. Without another word, he sharply jabbed the muzzles of his shotgun into the nearest knee. The result was instantaneous, and just as expected. With tears and snot flowing unchecked over his agonised features, the Metis suddenly couldn't stop talking.

'It was Dumont. Gabriel Dumont. She wouldn't lie with him, so he just shot her. And he enjoyed it. If he'd had more time, she'd really have suffered. I know him. I know what he's like. And all this was his idea. I just did what he told me to. I wouldn't ever hurt anyone.'

'Where are they all heading for now?' Bairstow demanded impatiently.

'I don't know,' the wounded man responded. Then his interrogator struck again, and the pathetic half-breed ended up in a foetal position, wailing in agony. '*S'il vous plaît, monsieur.* You have the truth. We were to split the money and scatter. Now, if you are chasing them, everything has changed.'

Before the Mountie could comment on that, the sound of shod hoofs came to his ears. He glanced around to see the marshal mounted and leading a spare horse. 'There isn't time for this,' that individual opined forcefully. 'We needs to be off, full chisel. Mustn't allow them time to force that strongbox and split up, 'cause two can't follow seven.'

Sense took over from raw anger, and Bairstow nodded his agreement. 'I guess.' So saying, he eased the shotgun's hammers down very carefully and then mounted the remaining horse.

The crew were chivvying reluctant male passengers over to the two discarded rails. As the lawmen swept past, Bronson called out, 'That bull turd's like to bleed out unless he gets some doctoring. It's your choice.' And then they were gone, any reply lost on the wind.

'So are they still after us?' Hatcher queried irritably. Somehow he knew what the answer would be.

Two hours had passed since leaving the stranded

train, and the seven men had been pushing their animals hard. They were travelling under a baking sun across seemingly endless grassland.

'They're out there, all right,' Carson replied as he scrutinised their back trail through his drawtube spyglass. 'Too far to be shot at, but close enough so as we don't get chance to work on the box.'

'Why don't we just wait for them?' Dumont demanded. 'Out in the open, we are seven to two, *oui?*'

'Maybe so,' Carson allowed. 'But they've both got scatterguns, and they know how to use them. As you've found out,' he added pointedly.

The Metis leader instinctively touched his superficial but painful flesh wound. Chaffed by the collar of his grubby shirt, it needed washing and dressing, but he had other things on his mind. 'Who is this Bronson that follows us?'

Hatcher spat in the dirt. 'He's a federal officer. A marshal. Tough son of a bitch, too. Works out of Billings, Montana. God knows what he's doing up here.'

Dumont favoured him with a suspicious glance. 'Maybe *your* presence has brought him amongst us. Have you thought of that?'

Carson sighed, and answered for his partner. 'Yeah, actually I had. But there ain't no point falling out over it. Nobody forced you to work with us. What we need to do is figure out how best to stop them. And if I *have* to kill them, I will, because I ain't seeing the inside of a cell ever again. And since you know

59

the land, you need to make the call.'

Dumont couldn't gainsay the logic in that. 'A place does come to me: a river crossing a little further to the north. It has many trees for cover. But first we should slow the pace. Killing these animals serves no purpose.'

Neither of the Americans could disagree with that. They had roped the heavy box to their saddle horns, and with that swinging between them their horses had a heavier burden than the others.

'I'll just settle for killing those law dogs,' Vern Hatcher snarled. 'Especially that Bronson. This ain't the first time he's darkened my trail, so it's past time we had a reckoning.'

Brin Carson wasn't the only one to possess a spyglass. The man who was tracking them was similarly equipped.

'We still keeping pace with them?' Bairstow demanded with a slight edge to his voice.

Bronson smiled to himself. He well knew that the Mountie envied his optical advantage. 'They've eased off a lot, and it makes sense. This could turn into one hell of a long pursuit. And whoever ends up afoot first gets to dying.' Then he gestured with his glass and added, 'This little toy really is all I can bring to the party at the moment. You know the land and the people. Just what are their intentions likely to be?'

Bairstow was mildly taken aback at the marshal's unaccustomed display of humility, but nonetheless he had answers ready. 'First off, I reckon they'll keep heading north. That way they'll keep well clear of the railroad, which only runs east/west. South would have taken them towards the border, which Dumont wouldn't want. While he's on his own ground, those two Americans will have to defer to him. A bit like with you and me,' he added slyly. 'My guess is they're making for the settlement of Saskatoon. It's around one hundred and thirty miles from Moose Jaw, and big enough for them to go to ground in. Who knows, he might even have friends there.' He paused, his bluff features suddenly pensive.

'What?' the other man demanded.

'Well, thing is, to get there, they have to cross the Qu'Appelle River. And therefore so will we. Problem is, they'll be there first. It's mostly deep and fast, with only the one crossing point for miles.'

Bronson caught on immediately. 'So if they're ever going to hit us, it'll be there.'

'Uh-huh. And there are plenty of trees along its banks for cover.'

'That's just swell. And yet if we don't cross, there'll be them on the one side and us on the other. We'll have us a regular Mexican standoff . . . only in Canada. *And* they'll be able to get to working on that box.'

'We do have one chance that occurs to me,' Bairstow ventured, his face now curiously devoid of expression. 'One of us crosses over in the dark, on foot, hopefully without being seen, and then the other comes over with the horses to flush them out. Neither task is particularly enviable.'

61

For the first time in years, Jesse Bronson was momentarily lost for words, but *only* momentarily. 'Hot dang!' he exclaimed. 'I wish I'd never asked. So it's either drown or get shot to pieces . . . or if we're really lucky, both at once!'

Six men were spread out in the undergrowth, whilst somewhere to their rear the seventh watched over the horses. Out in the wild, with known antagonists approaching, the animals were far too valuable a commodity to be trusted to picket pins alone. Likewise, the isolated horse herd guard couldn't be trusted with the strongbox. That lay mid-way between the Americans and Gabriel Dumont, who in turn didn't really trust either of them.

It was early evening. The sun was on the wane, and the ever-twitchy Vern Hatcher wasn't happy. 'If they were behind us, why the hell ain't they here yet?'

Carson glanced at him pityingly. Yes, they were *amigos*, but sometimes he really did despair of him a little. 'I don't know about the redcoat, but Bronson hasn't survived this long by being stupid. If he thinks we've camped by the river for the night, then he'll smell a trap and be wary about crossing over. He'll possibly decide to wait until tomorrow. Or he's maybe watching these trees through a spyglass of his own right now, waiting for us to start on the box. Sure, it's dark, but the noise alone would tip him off, which is why we ain't going to . . . yet!'

Dumont's hackles began to rise. 'This is my country, and these are my people. What makes you think you know so much?'

It was Hatcher who figuratively leapt to his partner's defence. 'Because he robs trains for a living and he's good at it. Real good. *And* he knows that damned marshal. You want to be rich, don't you? You've already got more cash money in your pockets than you ever had before, haven't you? So listen to him, and just maybe we'll all die in our beds, worn out by too much good living and too many bad women.'

Despite the tension between them, that tickled the Metis leader. 'Beds! I never been in no bed before. Not any kind. Ever!'

As he had known all along, it was Jesse Bronson who metaphorically drew the short straw. There was no other choice really. With only the one good hand, he couldn't both hold a weapon and control two horses on a river crossing in the dark. And so here he was, crouching in the undergrowth, next to a river the name of which he couldn't even pronounce.

Apart from maintaining his footing *and* not getting shot, his main task was to keep the sawn-off dry, or at least its ammunition. Thankfully, the days of cap an' ball weapons were long gone, but water and metallic cartridges could still be an unholy mix. Consequently, he had wrapped some in wax paper as a precaution. And knowing that he would need to be almost totally submerged to avoid detection, the marshal had handed his gun belt to Bairstow.

The Mountie was out of sight in the trees and, for

63

all Bronson could tell, the far bank might quite easily be deserted. Somehow, though, he knew that it wasn't. Yet luck was with him in one respect. Cloud had conveniently drifted over and obscured the moon, a situation that appeared likely to continue. Unusually for the summer months, it was therefore a genuinely dark night.

Sighing resignedly, he recognized that it was time to make his move. With the shotgun in the crook of his arms, Bronson crawled out of the long grass and down the gentle slope that lead to the Qu'Appelle. At this point it was some twenty yards across, and he had no real idea just how deep it was, because Bairstow's only recent crossing had been in winter. So much for local knowledge!

Slipping into the water came as a brutal shock that took his breath away. He hadn't expected it to be so cold, or for the current to be so strong. It was supposed to be summer, for Christ's sake!

Desperate to avoid splashes at all cost, he shifted the big gun to his right hand, and used the iron hook to gain traction on the riverbed. Soon his body was underwater, and he cursed the Mountie silently. This was definitely a job for a younger man.

As the depth increased, he got to his knees awkwardly, and then shortly after up into a standing crouch, with the chill water just below his nostrils. He was uncomfortably aware of the drag from his sodden clothes, and began to wonder whether he should have left those behind as well. Ahead lay the far bank, covered in trees and foliage. It was shrouded in darkness, which in truth was his only ally.

Expecting to receive a lethal hammer blow at any moment, he could feel the tension building in his frozen body. And yet, there was no alternative other than to keep plodding along the uneven river bottom, all the while praying that he wouldn't be discovered. And then, quite amazingly, he could feel the ground under him begin to angle up towards dry land. Perversely, even as his miserable journey came to an end, it was then that he was most vulnerable. Even if none of the outlaws had yet spotted him, he could quite easily stumble out of the river on top of one. Which was pretty much just about what happened!

Samuel Bairstow was only able to make out the top of Bronson's head above the water because he knew where to look. Failing to consider the possible dangers the marshal would run into when entering the undergrowth, the sergeant felt pretty confident that no one on the other bank was likely to discover his companion. And so, as the sodden shape finally crawled out of the Qu'Appelle River, he had already reluctantly decided that it was time to make his own crossing. Even with a hidden ally, the Mountie felt frighteningly vulnerable atop a horse. If he had known that that *ally* was actually in no position to help him, he would very probably have stayed put!

Away from the fearsome gaze of his leader, the Metis outlaw had been systematically lulled into a doze by the comforting effects of food in his belly and the sound of water lapping close by. Consequently, the sudden contact with a soaking apparition took him completely by surprise, which was exactly the same effect that *his* discovery had on Bronson. As that man's trembling body encountered the unseen human form, his heart lurched with shock. And yet tellingly, it was the American who reacted first. He had two weapons available, and instinctively he chose to use the iron hook that had years before replaced his left hand.

Sadly, the first blow failed to shatter a skull, but merely thumped against his victim's chest. That produced a grunt of pain, and then two hands defensively seized his forearm, pulling him sideways. So frenetic was their struggle that the half-breed hadn't yet managed to cry for help. Then, suddenly, everything happened at once.

Even as Sergeant Bairstow splashed into the river leading the marshal's horse, a voice hissed out a few yards from the frenziedly struggling men. 'Louis, what ails you?' Then, far louder, 'Jesus, they're here!'

Desperation seemed to lend Bronson strength, because he suddenly managed to arch his back and execute a great scything blow with his empty shotgun. Even as the solid butt smashed into his opponent's face, the lawman bellowed out, 'Dismount, Samuel!'

Whether his warning was in time, he had no way of knowing, because those words were barely out of his mouth before a volley of shots rang out.

Bairstow heard the familiar voice and reacted instantly. Falling to one side, he plunged into the cold water. Just like the American, minutes earlier, the chill took his breath away, but that was nothing to what he would have lost. The ragged fusillade crashed out before him, and immediately his recently acquired horse whinnied with pain. With his head barely above water, the Mountie glanced back in time to see the animal topple sideways and disappear under the surface. As more shots rang out in the undergrowth, he filled his lungs and plunged underwater. The weight of the shotgun, hanging from his neck by a strap, helped to take him down. The problem was, he couldn't stay there indefinitely, whereas the men waiting for him had no such constraints . . . or did they?

'Goddamn it!' Bronson snarled, and once more he lashed out with his big gun. Satisfyingly, it again struck home, and this time he heard the distinctive crack of breaking bone. Leaving his victim to suffer, he rolled twice, away from the riverbank. With more shots ringing out before him, he ripped open the wax paper packet and crammed two twelve-gauge cartridges into his shotgun. He had to make the risky assumption that anyone on land and behind a muzzle flash was an enemy. So depending on whether a horse holder had been appointed, he was likely up against five or six men. One thing was certain: he would need to keep moving.

A few yards away, a shot crashed out in the gloom. Reacting instantly, he aimed at the flash, discharged one barrel, and rolled clear again. His rapid movement was accompanied by a scream of pain from his latest victim, and suddenly Samuel Bairstow was no longer the sole focus of the outlaws' attention.

Brin Carson immediately recognized their predicament. 'We've been flanked!' he bellowed into the darkness.

With probably only a single assailant in amongst them with a scattergun, their superior numbers would now count against them. With their advantage lost, regrettably, they would have to hightail it, and fast. And with no time to secure the strongbox, he was about to find out just how robust it really was.

Grabbing hold of the rope attached to it, Carson scrambled away awkwardly from the river and towards the nervous horses. Dumont and his Metis trash could mix it with the lawmen whilst he took care of business, but he did take the trouble to alert his partner. And he did so in a way that was guaranteed to be unintelligible to their temporary accomplices.

'Boots and saddles, *compadre*!' he yelled whilst on the move. If Vern Hatcher didn't react to that, then he deserved to get shot!

The half-breeds' leader kept low to the ground as he waited for the shotgun to momentarily highlight its owner. In his right hand was the knife that had so terrified the railroad clerk in Regina. Frightened and confused, one of his remaining men cried out for instructions, but he ignored him. The ambush had deteriorated into chaos, but he had no intention of becoming the law dog's next victim.

His left hand closed over a piece of deadwood and he hurled it at the nearest tree. The explosive response was almost instantaneous. As black powder flared briefly in the night, Dumont launched himself towards its source, his honed blade ready to strike.

Ignoring the surviving, terrified horse as its floundering took it downriver and away, Bairstow dragged his sodden body out of the river just as Bronson's shotgun fired for the second time. The flash seemed to unleash a demonic knife-wielding figure from the undergrowth. There could be only one target for such an assault.

'Bronson, defend yourself!' he bellowed.

That man had kept one eye closed whilst shooting, and so retained some night vision. From the periphery of his left eye he spotted a vague shape lunging out of the darkness at him. Twisting to the side, Bronson raised his left arm instinctively as a shield. There was a bone-jarring crash as something metallic collided with his iron hook, and sparks flew. Before he could swing his shotgun around as a club, Dumont's body fell heavily onto him, knocking the marshal to the ground.

The knife had fallen from suddenly numbed

fingers, and the Metis cursed with frustration. Not having seen the marshal face to face during the hold-up, he could only assume that his knife had collided with some kind of firearm, rather than part of his body. In the dim light, he spotted the shotgun in his opponent's hand and knew that he couldn't allow that to be used against him as a club. Lunging forward, he seized the gun with both hands and tried to wrest it out of Bronson's grasp.

'*Cochon!*' he hissed venomously.

The American had no idea what that meant, and was in any case more concerned about losing his hold on the sawn-off. Yet he had one big advantage in any hand-to-hand fight that the half-breed was still oblivious to. Swinging his left arm up, he struck Dumont a glancing blow on the head with his iron hook that was nevertheless sufficient to send him reeling. Bronson took the opportunity to scrabble backwards, and then he kicked out with his right leg. His still sodden boot slammed into the other man's chest with tremendous force, sending him tumbling back into the undergrowth.

Breathing heavily from all the exertion, the marshal hastily reloaded his twelve-gauge and then peered around. Knowing that his companion had also survived the crossing, and was now out there in the dark, meant that any gunplay would have to be carefully controlled. And yet it suddenly appeared as though the outlaws were losing the desire to fight, because from a short distance away there came the sound of horses on the move. And that wasn't all.

70

'The Yankees are fleeing, Gabriel,' a heavily accented voice cried out from further along the bank. 'With the box!'

That disclosure was greeted by a momentary silence, and then another shotgun blasted out in the dark. Bairstow's contribution was followed by more screams and then an authoritative voice. 'Get to the horses, all of you.'

'*All of you*' turned out to be an exaggeration. Only two distinct footfalls sounded out as the survivors of the melee ran for their animals. There were then the sounds of a brief argument followed by pounding hoof beats that rapidly grew fainter. After that, all that could be heard was the keening sound of a wounded man somewhere in the undergrowth.

'You out there, Samuel?' Bronson tentatively enquired.

'Oh, yeah. I'm here all right,' came the reassuring response. Then, after a brief silence, he followed that with, 'So what do you think to my plan now?'

There was a short pause as the marshal got to his feet. 'Since I'm betting you've lost our horses *and* my old Remington, I'd have to say it could have panned out better. And unless they've left some of their animals behind again, this pursuit stops right now!'

CHAPTER SIX

It was a little over five years since John Fraser and his family had arrived in Saskatchewan from Edinburgh. That was of course Edinburgh, Scotland, and not New Edinburgh, Ottawa. Those five years had been long and gruelling. The Frasers had settled on one hundred and sixty acres of land, some twenty miles north of the Qu'Appelle River, and had hacked and scrapped at it from dawn until dusk, day in and day out. Their very survival hinged on successful harvests, and this year looked set to be a good one. The right combination of rain and sun, prayed for at the start of every meal, was ensuring that their crop would almost certainly be classed as Number 1 Northern Wheat at the market in Winnipeg. John had calculated that after maybe a couple more such harvests, they might even be able to replace their thoroughly unpleasant sod cabin with an expensive wooden frame house from back east. That was the dream, anyway.

The family had gathered for their midday meal in

the cabin, and with that now over were about to resume their various chores around the farm. John paused to gaze over at the great field of burgeoning wheat, and then at his wife and children. He smiled with pride and satisfaction. Laura, although prematurely aged by the harsh life, was still an exceptionally handsome woman. Well-made, with fine cheekbones and strawberry blonde hair, she never failed to make him wonder just how he had managed to woo her back in the old country.

The three children, two boys and a girl, were aged between nine and twelve. All old enough to pull their weight around the farm, thankfully: they had no chance of any formal education due to the complete lack of a schoolhouse within travelling distance. But what they lacked in learning, they made up for with a mostly healthy outdoor life that held the promise of eventual self-sufficiency for them all. It was the eldest, Angus, who first spotted the unexpected visitors approaching their property. He possessed excellent eyesight, but was unable to recognize any of the five horsemen.

'Those men are set to ride right through our wheat!' he exclaimed in amazement. No self-respecting farmer would ever dream of doing such a thing to his or anyone else's crops.

His father jerked in surprise. 'So they are, goddamn them!'

'John, don't cuss like that,' his wife admonished. Already, she had adopted some of the patois of their new homeland.

73

Ignoring her, Fraser angrily ran to the edge of the field and began to wave and shout at the now very unwelcome strangers. 'Move away from there, you fools. You'll damage the crop.'

For all the response he got, he might as well have not bothered. The five men continued their inexorable advance, trampling everything in their path. It was then that Fraser noticed certain things that were even more unsettling. One of them appeared to be injured, and only kept upright in his saddle by the support of a companion. *And* two others were carrying a large box of some kind between them. 'What on earth can that be?' he pondered to himself.

Something about their appearance definitely spooked Laura. 'Children, get inside,' she snapped. 'All of you.' Then, after a short pause, 'John, I think you should get your shotgun.'

Her mild-mannered husband blinked with surprise. Not once since they had taken possession of their acres had he been called upon to defend his land or family from either man or beast. But then he had never seen a band of men like these before. 'Perhaps you're right,' he acknowledged, turning on his heels and following his children inside.

It took the Scotsman some time to find the cartridges for his long-barrelled weapon, and by the time he emerged from the cabin the strangers had cut a swath through his field and were reining in before the sod building. Self-consciously retracting the hammers, Fraser moved forward to stand next to his wife. It was only then he realized he was confronted by an unusual mix of nationalities. Three of them, including one who was bleeding heavily, were Metis half-breeds. One of the two men holding the box gazed down at him with a half-smile playing on his lips. Although Fraser had never met any Americans, he decided that from their mode of dress they had to hail from the United States.

'You fixing on using that cannon, or what?' Brin Carson queried.

Something about the stranger's demeanour made the farmer nervous as hell, but he strove hard to conceal the fact. 'That depends on whether you intend to pay for the damage that you've caused,' he stated firmly.

'Damage,' Hatcher sneered. 'What damage?'

'To my wheat,' Fraser replied patiently but firmly. 'No man should ever trample another's crop.'

Dumont had already dismissed the sodbuster from his mind. It was the wife he was suddenly interested in. She looked like she'd led a hard life, but there was very obviously still enough juice left in her to stir his loins. 'Just kill him, and be done with it,' he barked.

A voice from behind distracted him abruptly, and temporarily took the heat out of the situation. 'Alain needs help, Gabriel,' the former horse holder insisted urgently. As if to reinforce that, the Metis wounded by Bairstow's shotgun blast groaned loudly.

Dumont signed irritably. The welfare of his men didn't normally rate so low, but lust had raised its ugly head again, effectively negating any rational thought. 'Oh very well,' he snapped. 'Get him off his horse. You people, fetch food, water and bandages. *Vite, vite.*'

Suddenly all was activity, and it left Fraser feeling flummoxed. First they wanted to kill him, and yet now they wanted his help. As the bleeding man was assisted to the ground, the farmer glanced at his wife. 'Best do as they say, but keep the children inside.'

Laura turned away to comply reluctantly, leaving him with his shotgun still readied but no real idea what to do with it. Then the two men holding the box lowered that to the ground, and the one who had spoken first peered at him from under the rim of his wide brimmed hat.

'Don't seem like there's another spread for miles, which means you must have some blacksmith's tools around here somewhere. How's about you fetch them so's my partner and I can get to work on this box?'

Fraser possessed stubbornness typical of the Scots. He didn't like being ordered around on his own property. But then the other man made as if to swat a fly away, and quite amazingly, a revolver appeared in his hand. It was cocked and aimed directly at John Fraser. The speed had been breathtaking.

'But before you do that,' the American continued conversationally, 'Why don't you just lower those hammers, real careful like, and put that gun on the deck. Then we can do what we have to do, and get on about our business without any of you coming to harm.'

Fraser stared at him for a moment before acquiescing grudgingly. It was dawning on him that if he was ever to have stood a chance of holding these marauders off, then he should have forted up in the cabin and opened fire the moment they got close. Except that life wasn't like that on the Canadian Plains. Visitors had always proved to be friendly, and welcomed as such.

With the shotgun on the ground, Fraser headed for the barn, the cost of which had taken all his remaining savings when they first arrived. In there, he had all the tools required for shoeing a horse . . . or forcing a stolen strongbox open. As he walked away, he heard the man referred to as Gabriel snigger. 'You're real fast with that pistol, ain't you?'

'Best you remember it come time to divvy up,' Carson replied shortly.

Then Laura appeared with a bowl of water, and cloth for bandages, and the Metis's attention was suddenly elsewhere. Unaware of his lustful eyes roaming over her body, she carefully examining her whimpering patient, and finally shook her head grimly. 'This man needs more than just cleaning up,' she avowed. 'These pellets need digging out, or the wounds will infect. And that's if he doesn't bleed to death first.'

'Then you'd better get to it, hadn't you?' Vern Hatcher remarked. 'Because if he ain't fit to ride when we move on, you'll have yourself a house guest. An' we ain't got time to hang around, 'cause those law dogs are sure to be on our heels.'

Laura didn't even react to that admission, because the fact that these men were fugitives from the law came as no surprise. Instead, she began the tortuous

77

task of removing lead shot from her patient piece by bloody piece. With no anaesthetic or even hard liquor available, it was set to be a gruesome task.

As anguished cries rent the air, Carson tilted his hat back to wipe sweat from his forehead. 'It's hot as Hades out here. Let's shift this box into the barn.' Then he glanced at Dumont. 'Don't go fussing yourself. We won't be palming any off on the side.'

Strangely, considering his venal nature, the Metis didn't seem particularly concerned. The sight of Laura, now perspiring heavily, meant that his attention was very definitely elsewhere, and that should have been warning enough for the others. The Americans had both witnessed his brutal treatment of the young brunette on the train. As it was, they merely picked up the box between them and followed the farmer into his barn.

'Och, but that's well put together,' John Fraser opined. 'It's going to take some work to break into it.'

'That's why it's called a *strongbox*,' Carson retorted dryly. 'An' as my partner here said, we ain't got all day, so you'd better get to it.'

Unenthusiastically, the sodbuster set to work with a hammer and chisel. And yet lacklustre effort wasn't his way, so he was soon going at it with gusto. It wasn't long before the first padlock fell away. Things were at last looking up for the impatient outlaws. Then there came a deal of shouting, followed by a high-pitched scream that bore no resemblance to the agonised cries of the wounded Metis.

'Oh, Christ, now what?' Carson demanded angrily.

Fraser knew *what*. His wife was in serious trouble and the possibilities overwhelmed him. 'Laura!' he exclaimed. Dropping his tools like hot coals, he brushed past the startled Americans without any consideration for his own safety and raced outside. The vision he beheld was the stuff of nightmares.

In front of the cabin, where his horrified children were staring through the open door, his beloved spouse lay on the ground next to her patient, writhing in a growing pool of her own blood. Next to her stood the somewhat bemused figure of Gabriel Dumont, a bloody knife clutched in his right hand. Catching sight of her distraught husband, he merely shrugged. The only thing that occurred to him was that he hadn't been faring very well with women of late.

'What have you done?' Fraser howled.

'The bitch tried to stick me with that cutting tool,' the half-breed retorted, indicating the knife that she had been using to extract the lead shot.

Almost beside himself with grief, the farmer charged over to his stricken wife. Dropping to his knees, he cradled her tenderly in his arms for a moment. Then, frantically pressing down on her wound, he attempted to stem the bleeding, but it was all to no avail. With her unseeing eyes locked on his, she drifted away slowly.

'Now why would she have done a thing like that, Dumont?' Carson asked, a hint of menace noticeable in his voice. 'Was it because you were trying to get in her skirts . . . even while she was helping your man there?'

'What if I was?' the other man sneered. 'What's it to you?'

Carson sighed. 'What is it with you and women? D'you only like the ones who struggle?'

Dumont leered at him. 'They all struggle . . . at first. But this one, she was like a vixen.'

That proved to be too much for the American. 'You kill crazy son of a bitch. When this is all over, we go our own separate ways . . . permanently. You hear? Vern an' me came up here to get rich, not see you butcher every woman we come across!'

The Metis's brow furrowed. His knife hand drifted towards his holstered six-gun. Then he recalled the dazzling speed with which Carson had drawn on Fraser, and he froze.

The American favoured him with an icy smile. 'Anytime you want, mister.'

It was at that moment that Fraser's grief turned to rage. 'You murdering bastard!' he roared, and rushed for his discarded shotgun. Dumont would have shot him dead willingly, except that he was wary of drawing his gun in case it provoked a lethal response from Carson. As it was, that man had other ideas.

'Cold cock him, Vern,' he snapped.

Moving fast, Hatcher intercepted Fraser just as that individual reached the big gun. Drawing his revolver so that he held it by the barrel, he brought the butt down solidly on Fraser's skull. The Scotsman grunted once and went down like a sack of grain.

'It would have been just as easy to kill him,' a puzzled Hatcher remarked.

Carson shook his head emphatically, and then gestured towards the terrified children. 'I'll kill any *man* that gets in my way, but I ain't making orphans of those three just for the hell of it!'

Hatcher shrugged. 'Well, either way, I guess we'll just have to open that damn box ourselves.'

'Maybe not, mister,' commented the only remaining uninjured Metis gang member as he pointed off down their back trail.

All eyes turned to the south. Out on the distant horizon, two tiny figures were just visible to those with sharp eyes. Of course they could have been anybody, but wishful thinking was a luxury that none of them could afford.

'Goddamn it all to hell,' Carson exclaimed. 'It's like having the grim reaper on our tail.'

'Now what?' Hatcher queried.

'We take the box *and* the tools and get the hell out of here. That's what.' Then he glanced pointedly at Dumont. 'Yeah?'

The half-breed stared at him for a long moment, and then finally allowed the tension to ebb from his body. 'Yeah.'

'What about Alain?' queried the other Metis, looking to his leader.

Again it was Carson who answered that. 'He stays here. There's no room for passengers on this trip. Whether he lives or dies will be up to the sodbuster

81

. . . when he wakes up. It'll be his choice whether he takes a life for a life. I reckon you owe him that much,' he added with a sharp glace at Dumont. Then, that business concluded, he turned on his heels and waved Hatcher back to the barn.

Gabriel Dumont stared at them in sullen silence. Abandoning another fellow Metis didn't sit well with him, and his patience with the overbearing Yankees was in any case wearing very thin. If they ever shook off their deadly shadows, then there would definitely have to be a reckoning. It didn't occur to his fevered mind that such dark thoughts were no longer original, or that every time they came to him, his band of followers had dwindled further!

CHAPTER SEVEN

As a long-serving federal officer, Jesse Bronson had come upon many a scene of death and misery in his time, and if this one wasn't the most unpleasant, then it sure would do until something worse came along.

Sprawled in front of the sod cabin, apparently drenched in her own blood, lay a woman in a long cotton dress. A cursory glance was sufficient to determine that her once handsome features were now waxy and totally devoid of life. Of the three children visible, the two youngest were weeping over her still form. The eldest, a boy, was huddled next to his father who appeared to be recovering from a blow to the head. Close by, a moaning figure apparently liberally peppered with shot lay abandoned by his cronies.

'Looks like you actually managed to hit something with that scattergun of yours,' the marshal commented dryly as he urged his latest captured animal over towards the shattered family.

The Mountie grunted unhappily. He took no pleasure in shooting people, and his career north of the border had generally involved far less bloodshed than of late. Tellingly, the amount of violence that he encountered always seemed to increase when he was in Bronson's company. The body count on their previous foray together had been truly staggering. 'If your felons stayed in their own country, I wouldn't even need the poxy thing,' he retorted.

As the lawman from Montana reined in by the groggy farmer from Scotland and then dismounted slowly, Angus Fraser peered anxiously up at him. Uncovering his marshal's shield, Bronson gruffly demanded, 'What happened here, boy? Speak up. I'm a lawman. You've nothing to fear from us.'

Haltingly, tearfully, the youngster related the terrible happenings. The shocked expression on his previously innocent face served to add depressing power to the grim tale.

'And they rode off with the strongbox still unopened?' the peace officer prompted.

Although obviously bewildered by such a question, Angus nodded his agreement.

'Then we need to keep pushing them,' Bronson remarked to his companion. 'That box will both slow them down and keep them together.'

'And I'll be coming with you,' John Fraser suddenly announced in his still distinctive Scottish accent. It would take more than five years of absence from the old country to erase that.

Bairstow recoiled in surprise. 'I'm sorry, mister,

but that's just not possible. This red jacket tells you that I'm a sergeant in the Mounted Police. It's *my* job to apprehend those men, and I just can't allow a civilian to be endangered.'

With his son's help, Fraser had finally got back on his feet. His head was throbbing like an anvil strike, but next to the enormity of his loss that was nothing. '*Endangered* is it?' he roared with uncharacteristic anger. 'And what do you call the murder of my wife?'

Momentarily lost for words, the Mountie could only stand there and accept the justified tirade.

'You weren't here to save Laura from those butchers,' the farmer continued, tears now flowing freely down his cheeks. 'But I'll be there when you catch up with them to see she's avenged one way or another! Or doesn't her death mean anything to you?'

Despite the circumstances, Samuel Bairstow flushed angrily. Moving closer, until he was face-to-face with the distraught Scotsman, he replied, 'One of those same men shot my wife in the back because she wouldn't lay with him. Right now, I don't know whether she's alive or dead, because I'm out here trying to catch those cockchafers. And we'll do it, too. They were nine strong at the start, and now they're down to five, if you can count him,' he added, gesturing dismissively at the gravely wounded man. Then he paused and drew in a deep breath. It occurred to him that he would very probably regret what he was about to say. 'Very well. You can come with us, but we're in charge. Understand? *We are in charge!* You don't even belch without our say so. And if you can't keep up, you'll be left behind.'

Startled at the policeman's revelation, Fraser just nodded dumbly, before asking abruptly, 'What's your wife's name?'

'Kirsty.'

It was Angus who cut off any possible response to that. He didn't give a damn about someone else's wife. His mother was dead, and apparently his father was about to ride off with two more complete strangers. There was an edge of hysteria to his voice as he demanded shrilly, 'But what about us, Papa? And what about the harvest? You can't just up and leave us.'

Fraser patted his shoulder sadly but resolutely. 'Och, to the devil with the wheat, lad. With your mother gone, it means nothing anymore. There's not anything can bring her back, but the murdering scum that killed her will answer before God for his foul act. And you are the eldest, so you will have to be strong, for the sake of your brother and sister.' He glanced at Bairstow. 'You're . . . *we* are riding north after those cutthroats, yes?'

'Uh-huh.'

'So we'll take the children to the Duffields on the way. It's the next farm in that direction. They are fine, God-fearing people. They'll look after them while I'm gone.'

Bronson, for one, wasn't convinced about the farmer's prospects. 'And what if *you* don't make it back? What happens to the youngsters then?'

Fraser had no answer for that, and so turned away

86

to see to the other children. They were eerily quiet, as though numbed by the inexplicable violence. 'We must bury Laura,' was all he could manage. The poor man was painfully aware that he might not be present when his bairns were finally struck by the terrible reality of all that had passed.

The marshal shrugged, and then pointed at the suffering Metis. 'An' what about this sack of shit?'

Bairstow was ready for that, and his answer showed that the American wasn't the only one with a hard edge. 'Leave him to take his chances, like we did with the other one at the river. He looks hurt bad, and like to die. Even if he doesn't, he'll have plenty of time to reflect on his bad deeds. And one thing's for sure, he won't be robbing any more trains.'

'Sweet Jesus!' Carson exclaimed as he sat his horse at the crest of a slight rise. There was a creak of well-worn saddle leather as he shifted position. 'There's three of the bastards now. They're becoming more as we get less!'

Hatcher grabbed the spyglass from him and squinted against the bright light. 'The grieving sodbuster's joined them. You should have let me kill him when I had the chance.'

The other man shrugged. 'Maybe so, but there's no point getting into "if onlys". What we need to do is get an edge.'

'But to get that, you need to know the land and its people,' Gabriel Dumont suddenly observed. 'And I do.'

The Americans glanced at him in surprise. The half-breed had been very quiet since they'd all fled the Fraser homestead some hours before, not even talking to his single remaining follower.

'Can't argue with that,' Carson allowed. 'So what's your local knowledge telling you?'

Labeau regarded him steadily. 'It tells me that there is a Cree village a few miles from here. They used to camp around Moose Jaw, until the Canadian Pacific arrived and the settlers that followed ran them off. Which means that they don't much like anyone who works for the railroad.'

'And just how does that help us?' Hatcher retorted. Carson, however, was already nodding his head in appreciation.

'Many of my kind are related to the Cree,' Labeau continued. 'The leader will know of me and listen to what I have to say. So I'll do what you white men have always done with *uncivilized* Indians: lie to them!'

The uninitiated thought that the great Northern Plains, which stretched across a sizeable chunk of both southern Canada and the higher latitudes of the United States, were just flat and featureless throughout, but this was far from the truth. There were undulations and creases in the land that allowed the skilful to remain hidden, should they so choose. And, although the white man's inexorable progress across land that they now considered to be theirs had almost destroyed the Indians' way of life, the Cree still retained their skills as warriors when

88

the need arose – as they were about to demonstrate.

The three-man posse was pushing on, with apparently open country on all sides. Bronson and the farmer were to the fore, riding side by side, whilst Bairstow followed on behind, pretty much hidden from anyone facing them. The single gunshot quite obviously came from directly ahead, it being impossible to hide black powder smoke on such a clear day. The bullet slammed into the chest of Fraser's horse, causing its front legs to buckle, and pitching him forward into the long grass. His two companions reacted with practised speed.

Since abandoning the farmer and fleeing wasn't an option, both of them dismounted, and by applying pressure to their animals forelegs were able to bring both creatures to the ground. As blood spurted from the fatal wound in Fraser's mount, Bronson bellowed out to him, 'If you're still awake, stay down and cock your piece. Whoever it is means business!'

Despite the jarring shock, the farmer was still conscious and did as instructed, even having the sense to fort up behind his dying horse. It was then that a band of half-naked copper-toned riders suddenly burst into view. Howling out unintelligible insults, they swept around the three white men at dazzling speed, but made no attempt to close in. Bairstow stared at them intently for a moment. Bronson had levelled his Winchester, which his companion had somehow saved from the clutches of the Qu'Appelle river, and was about to start drawing blood when he received a very unusual command.

'Fire over their heads,' the Mountie instructed. 'Or at the ground. Just don't hit anyone.'

'Are you crazy?' the marshal retorted. 'They're out to lift our scalps for sure!'

'Just do it, for God's sake!' came the reply. 'It's not the Wild West up here. We're civilised.'

'You could have fooled me,' the American scoffed, but nonetheless aimed high as he began to fire at the circling Indians.

Still dazed, Fraser merely looked on in fearful amazement. Like every other relatively new arrival on the continent, he had heard lurid tales of past conflicts with various Indian tribes, mostly south of the border, but never in his wildest imaginings had he ever expected to get caught up in one.

It was as Bronson blazed away ineffectually that Bairstow took careful and deliberate aim with his own Winchester. His particular target was the leader of the apparent war party, but his intentions were far from deadly. With his iron sights lined up on the Crees' piebald pony, he timed his shot to perfection. The bullet struck the animal's chest, bringing it and its rider crashing to the ground in exactly the same fashion as had occurred to Fraser.

'One rule for us, an' another for you, eh?' Bronson observed acidly as he ceased firing. 'Just what the hell are you about?'

With their leader suddenly brought low, his warriors milled about him in confusion. Bairstow heaved a great sigh of relief when he witnessed the man stagger uncertainly to his feet. That individual's death would definitely have brought forth unknown consequences. As it was, his survival meant that it was now time to proceed with the second, and far more dangerous part of his plan.

'Cover me,' he ordered as he abruptly allowed his struggling animal to return upright. He then proceeded to do the exact opposite of what common sense dictated. Mounting up, he brushed down the scarlet jacket and then fastened the top buttons. He next tilted his wide-brimmed hat to a more rakish angle, before returning the Winchester to its scabbard. The sawn-off was better suited for what he had in mind. Especially if the tide turned against him!

'You've gone plumb loco,' Bronson exclaimed. 'Get down from there, before they blow you off!'

'Watch and learn, Deputy,' Bairstow replied with a great deal more confidence than he was actually feeling. So saying, he spurred his animal into motion and moved directly towards the band of Indians.

The farmer from Edinburgh had never seen anything like it in his life. 'What on earth is he doing? Why don't you stop him?' he demanded of the marshal.

Bronson merely shrugged. He was beginning to discern the Canadian's strategy . . . and besides, 'It's not easy reining him in when the mood takes him. Believe me, I've tried.'

And so the two men remained in place, one hiding behind his now dead horse, the other laying across the neck of his, whilst squinting down the barrel of his rifle. If Bairstow's scheme all went wrong, then the marshal would at least take a few of their assailants with him.

Sergeant Samuel Bairstow of the Northwest Mounted Police had never felt more vulnerable in his life. The entire Cree war party had turned to watch his bold approach. Some were shouting imprecations and waving their weapons. The urge to flee was almost overwhelming, and yet, as he drew closer, he began to notice certain telltale things that spoke volumes. The ponies appeared to be scrawny and poorly cared for. Likewise, the warriors looked unkempt and undernourished, as though all was not well with their people. They possessed an air of desperation, rather than brooding menace. Like the Sioux and others of their kind, these men were no longer the vaunted warriors of the Plains. Their spirit had been irrevocably broken by disease, starvation and quite possibly something else as well.

As he knew it would be, his imposing red jacket was now the sole focus of the Indians' attention, and mercifully their demeanour became less threatening. They saw him for what he was, and it occurred to him that they had very probably only opened fire in the first place because they hadn't spotted his uniform as he rode in the rear. Finally, he reined in before them and gazed imperiously down at the unhorsed leader. That man, nervously flicking at imaginary flies with a quirt made from elk antler and leather, glanced at the chevrons on his arms, before belatedly making the sign of peace.

The Mountie responded in kind, before entering

into a mishmash dialogue of sign language, Pidgin English and corrupted French. Under other circumstances, what he discovered would have made him chuckle. As it was, the two men agreed that the unnecessary encounter had cost each side equally, but nevertheless Bairstow issued him with a stern warning: Queen Victoria's redcoats would not tolerate any such behaviour in the future, regardless of who was involved. *He* had spoken. This was Canada, not the United States, where conflict between the two sides had been commonplace.

Throughout the parley, the mounted policemen had ostentatiously kept his sawn-off on display. Now, as a sign of trust, he lowered the hammers and then backed his horse up with great skill, so as to maintain eye contact with the leader. Then he sat, silent and grave, and waited for the Crees to depart. This was a very deliberate display of authority, designed to demonstrate his position as the government's appointed representative. Only when they were some distance away did he finally return to his companions.

'God knows, a Scot has no love of redcoats,' John Fraser remarked, 'but I've never seen the like of that before.'

'I've got to admit, you sure can put on a show,' Bronson agreed. 'Just what was all that about, anyhu?'

For the first time in quite a while the Mountie smiled broadly, as much from the relief of having survived than anything he had to impart. 'The chief said a Metis going by the name of Gabriel Dumont came to them, and told them that we were surveyors for the Canadian Pacific Railroad. Apparently the three of us are the forerunners of a new stretch of track coming up from Regina. The slaughter of the buffalo and the arrival of the railroad have destroyed their way of life, so it's not surprising they got mad. That murdering bastard Dumont has got one hell of a lot to answer for.' He paused thoughtfully for a moment, and the others waited in silence as though sensing that there was more to come. 'There was something else as well. Those Indians were fired up by more than just Dumont's lies. They'd been drinking. I could smell the cheap rotgut on them, and that would tie in with the rumours that I've been hearing recently. Someone's selling whiskey to the tribes.' Bairstow fell quiet as he turned to watch the Indians fade gradually from view.

'So why didn't you ask them who's doing it?' Bronson queried.

The Mountie glanced at him. 'Because they weren't in any mood for questions about such things, and I wanted to keep my scalp, that's why.' It was then that another matter occurred to him, and he turned to gaze apologetically at the farmer. 'I'm real sorry about your horse, John, but what's done is done. You'll have to double up with one of us ... won't he, *Marshal*?'

Bronson stared at him askance. 'Why me?'

The Mountie smiled again, rather enjoying his ascendancy. 'Because those Cree might still be around. You can never be sure with Indians. And they quite rightly see me as possessing much power. It wouldn't look correct for one such as me to share a horse.'

The American shook his head. 'Huh. *One such as me*, is it? If I'd known you were so important, I'd have kept six paces behind from the start!'

Nevertheless, he reached down to assist Fraser in climbing up behind him, and the three men resumed their pursuit. What they now lacked in speed would likely be more than compensated for by the fact that the fugitives would consider them to be out of the hunt entirely.

CHAPTER EIGHT

Shadows flickered eerily in the small grove of trees next to the burbling creek. The four men had eaten and drunk their fill, and now their thoughts were turning to other, more mercenary matters. Not everyone was content with the situation, however.

'I tell you, this fire is a piece of goddamn foolishness,' Brin Carson protested. 'What with that and the smell of food, we might just as well run an ad.'

Dumont peered at him over the edge of his coffee cup. He did just wonder if these Yankees ever shut up, but contented himself with a mild retort. 'Those two law dogs will be crow bait by now. And we didn't even have to waste any more cartridges. Just accept that I did good.'

Amazingly, even Hatcher appeared to be convinced, and he also couldn't resist cracking a joke. 'I thought you said those scalp-lifters were Cree not Crow!' As the others groaned and rolled their eyes, he continued with, 'Anyhu, I think he's got the right of it, Brin. You heard all the shooting. Bronson and that redcoat couldn't have stood off the whole war party. And as for that sodbuster, he probably just shit his britches. Those Injuns'll likely be feeding his *cojones* to their squaws right about now. Such things are a delicacy for them.'

'That old bastard's got nine lives,' muttered Carson, but even so, his eyes began to drift towards the strongbox. 'But I guess if we are gonna light up the night sky like it's Independence Day, then we might as well make good use of it. Bring those tools over here.'

His partner complied eagerly, and soon they were all on their knees around the box, encouraging Carson to strike out ever harder. Working towards a common objective, the atmosphere was even becoming noticeably more companionable. After a few moments of vigorous hammering, a padlock fell to the ground, its hackle irrevocably smashed out of line. There were plenty more yet, along with some particularly impressive steel bars, but at last they were making progress. The four men could almost smell the money, and even Carson was showing signs of animation.

'The effort this is taking will just make the spending of all that *dinero* even more fun,' he commented gleefully.

The bullet glanced off the edge of the strongbox with a resounding clang, before ricocheting off into the trees, narrowly missing one of the tethered horses. Another rifle discharged, its projectile kicking up sparks and ashes from the campfire. Then

97

a shotgun crashed out in the night, emitting a massive muzzle flash, and Dumont's remaining follower screamed with pain. The outlaws grabbed their guns to return fire, but theirs was a very one-sided task. Sure, there had been powder flashes to aim at, but any professional worth his salt would have moved immediately after firing. There was also another concern to attend to.

Reacting fast, Carson grabbed hold of the strong-box and dragged it squarely onto the small cooking fire, smothering it instantly. No longer backlit, the three functioning outlaws spread out amongst the trees, but they were still at a disadvantage, and recognized the fact.

'Surrender, you sons of bitches, or it'll go badly for you,' the marshal from Montana bellowed.

'Go to hell, Bronson,' Hatcher hollered back. 'That badge don't mean doodly squat up here.'

'Maybe not, but my uniform does as well you know,' Bairstow countered. 'And it certainly impressed that Cree war party, *Gabriel.* So which'll it be?'

'We deal in lead, redcoat scum,' Dumont bellowed back, before squeezing off a shot. He had little expectation of hitting anyone, but raw anger mixed with a large dose of frustration was coursing through his veins. He'd no idea how these law dogs had eluded the war party, but they certainly had no business hounding him in this way. His cronies from south of the border obviously felt the same, because they too blazed away ferociously for some moments before common sense and empty magazines prevailed.

The wounded Metis continued to scream his guts out, and with the sudden lull in shooting the awful sound worked on Hatcher's nerves something terrible. 'Somebody shut him up, for Christ's sake. I can't think straight.'

'That's never stopped you before,' Dumont snarled at him, their recent affability entirely forgotten.

The American's response to that was lost in another burst of firing from beyond the grove of trees. Bullets and smaller pieces of lead shot thudded into wood, and it could only be a matter of time before someone else was hit.

'We can't stay here,' hissed Carson. 'They've got us surrounded. Even if we last until daylight they'll pick off the horses, and then we'll be in real trouble.'

Dumont fumed silently. He knew the Yankee was right, because he always seemed to be . . . Goddamn him. 'All right,' he agreed. 'We will leave this place.'

'See if your man can stop wailing long enough to cover us,' the American replied. 'Vern an' me will bring the box.'

'What is it with you Americans?' Dumont angrily demanded. 'I'm not leaving yet *another* man behind. He is one of my people, and we watch out for each other. Is that not so in your *United* States?'

Carson had been about to loose off a shot, but instead returned his full attention to the Metis. 'That kind of depends on who it is. That fella ain't said more than six words this whole trip. I don't even know his name, so I ain't about to risk *my* life for him.'

'He is called Gaspard.'

'Well, good for him,' Carson retorted, privately considering that he'd never heard such a ridiculous moniker. 'So do as you please. We've got our hands full with this box.' So saying, he unleashed a withering fire into the darkness with his Winchester. Working the under-lever like a berserker, he moved the barrel back and forth in a lateral arc, only stopping when the repeater finally dry fired. Then he scurried over to join Hatcher by the makeshift fireplace, and together they carried the battered strongbox through the trees to the horses. The tools stolen from Fraser's farm lay abandoned near the extinguished fire. They would have to be replaced in Saskatoon . . . if they made it that far.

Dropping onto all fours, Dumont crawled over to determine Gaspard's condition. That individual's screams had subsided into a continuous low moan. Either his strength was failing or maybe the pain was easing off. Fresh blood glistened on his upper body, but it was impossible to discern his real condition.

'Listen to me,' the Metis leader rasped. 'We cannot stay here. I will help you to your horse. Then you will either ride or die. *Qui?*'

The other man merely grunted, but Dumont felt sudden massive pressure on his right arm as Gaspard seized hold. The will to live was obviously still strong, and together they got him to his feet. With his leader half carrying him, the wounded man made it through the few scattered trees to his animal. There they found the Americans mounted up, and with the strongbox again suspended between them. It occurred to the Metis that if they were not careful, the cursed thing would surely bring about the death of them all.

As though emphasizing that fact, a shotgun again crashed out to their rear, and pellets could quite literally be heard smacking through leaves and foliage. Gaspard's horse whinnied in fear and struggled to pull free.

'Let's get the hell out of here,' Hatcher yelled, and dug his heels in savagely. As his horse lurched forward, Carson had no alternative other than to follow on, or risk being dragged from his mount. That left Dumont alone to assist Gaspard up into his swaying saddle. '*Cochons!*' he swore angrily.

Finally they were both mounted, and side-by-side with one supporting the other, they rode off in the Americans' wake.

The sound of pounding hoofs was only just audible as the three men came together amongst the trees. After all the gunfire, the sudden quiet felt strangely ominous.

'Are we to chase them?' John Fraser asked eagerly. His pulse was still racing from the thrill of the firefight, enhanced all the more by the fact that none of them had been injured. And it had been pellets from his shotgun blast that had struck the anguished Metis.

101

The two lawmen eyed each other in the gloom. Bronson emphatically shook his head, but let the Canadian have his say. After all, it was his country.

'I reckon not,' that man opined. 'A horse could too easily break a leg in the dark. Especially one with two riders on its back. We'll rest up for a while in these same trees, and fill the canteens with some fresh creek water.'

That prospect rapidly dampened Fraser's fervour. 'But what if they double back and attack us? We'd be in the same position that they were. Or what if they keep on going and we lose them? I won't just stand by and let Laura's killer get clean away!'

Bronson chuckled. 'Hot dang, sodbuster, you're full of "what ifs" tonight, ain't you?'

'Don't seem likely, either way,' Bairstow continued, ignoring the American and addressing Fraser's concerns. 'They've got a wounded man and a strongbox to tote around. That'll restrict their movements a mite. And as for losing them . . . Well, that ain't going to happen, since I'm pretty damn sure where they're heading. And that's Saskatoon, because as I told the marshal earlier, there's nowhere else out here of any size.'

'What possible delights can that place hold, I wonder?' Bronson pondered rhetorically. He was no stranger to tough frontier towns, and it was a sad fact that you could never quite predict what such a place might throw at you!

CHAPTER NINE

In many ways Saskatoon was like any other recently minted frontier town. Wide dirt streets lined by mostly hastily thrown-up buildings, with no running water and little sanitation. Yet in one way it was very unusual, in that it possessed no saloons or dancehalls of any kind. Established a few years earlier as a 'dry' community by the Methodist-backed Temperance Colonisation Society of Toronto, it had grown up on the banks of the same Qu'Appelle River that the marshal had crossed on his northbound pursuit. John Lake, the original founder, had travelled west to Moose Jaw by railroad, and then north by horse-drawn cart. Under his firm hand, the community had expanded rapidly in the growing prairie region, but many of the people who now resided there were far from ideal citizens.

One such individual happened to be idling away the hot morning with a little whittling as he hunkered down on a wooden sidewalk outside the general store, when an interesting sight abruptly claimed all his attention.

'Hey, Lash,' he called back into the interior. 'Something here you ought to see.'

'Such as?' came the unenthusiastic response.

'Four strangers riding in: I reckon they're outlawed up. One of them's busted up real bad . . . and they've got some kind of *strongbox* with them.'

A chair dragged noisily, and then rapid footsteps sounded in the single-room cabin. The fellow who appeared at the threshold was a monster of a man. Well over six feet tall with shoulders like house sides, his unshaven features were unremittingly brutal in appearance. Hard eyes took in the newcomers speculatively. Since they were now almost level with him, he could not actually see the strongbox, but nevertheless his interest had been secured. Ruled by greed, the storeowner began to consider his options immediately. Because one way or another, hard or easy, he would see to it that he got his hands on whatever was inside. At that very moment, as though sensing his malevolent purpose, one of the two lead riders abruptly turned and stared intently at the two observers for a few moments.

'D'you know him?' the sidewalk idler enquired in strangely hushed tones.

'No, but I reckon I'm going to,' Lash replied ominously, as he watched the four horsemen continue slowly down the main street. 'Go find Tector. Tell him I've got a job for him. And don't take "no" for an answer, even if he's riding some whore!'

*

The four new arrivals had certain specific require-
ments, and logically the first place to start had to be
the livery stables. The horses needed tending to, and
it would be an unobtrusive place in which to attend
to other needs, so long as an accommodation could
be reached with the operator. As one of the most
important businesses in town, the livery was naturally
situated on the main street, a short distance away
from the two observers and on the opposite side. It
was easily the largest of all the mostly timber struc-
tures that lined the thoroughfare.

'That big, ugly cuss seemed awful interested in us,'
Hatcher remarked to his partner. 'D'you know him?'

'No, but I've a feeling I'm going to,' Carson
replied somewhat fatalistically. It was beginning to
seem as though trouble with a capital 'T' had
attached itself to them permanently.

As the dusty and very weary horsemen reined in
outside their destination, the two Americans lowered
the strongbox to the ground gratefully, and dismounted swiftly. Behind them, Gabriel Dumont
helped his man out of the saddle. Only instinct and
an iron will had prevented Gaspard from toppling
out of it on the gruelling journey.

It being a warm day, the big double doors were
already wide open. Eager to get their prize away from
inquisitive eyes, Carson and Hatcher released it from
their saddle horns, grabbed the handles and carried
it inside. The twin odours of hay and horseflesh were
instantly recognizable.

'Can I help you fellas?' The voice was not

unfriendly, and emanated from a stooped old-timer with bushy sideburns and yellow teeth. He peered wide-eyed at the potential customers and their unusual load, but that was nothing to his expression when Dumont staggered in supporting Gaspard.

'You the owner?' Carson queried.

'Hell, no,' the stable-hand retorted with a wheezy laugh. 'That'd be Mister Harriman, but he's out of town on a hunting trip.'

'A hunting trip, huh,' the American reflected. 'So what do they call you?'

'Name's Toby. I kind of run things here . . . when Mister Harriman's away, that is. On account of I'm the oldest, I guess.' While speaking, his eyes lingered searchingly on Carson's travel-stained features as though trying to recall some other time and place.

After a brief survey of the spacious premises, which took in two young fellas shovelling shit and forking hay in the background, Carson's gaze settled on the diminutive employee. 'Well I'll tell you, Toby, this is your lucky day. We've got us a long list of wants. For starters, we've got four well-used animals that need stalls and attention. This fella needs a saw-bones, and I want some blacksmith's tools. You do have a blacksmith, don't you?'

Toby's eyes had narrowed. He plainly didn't like the look of the half-breeds, or the blood that was seeping from one of them. 'That'd be Mister Harriman as well, but as I already told you, he's . . .'

'Yeah, yeah. Out of town, I know,' Carson retorted, impatience entering his tone.

'But he'd have a smithy, yeah?' Hatcher chipped in. 'So we could just up and borrow the tools. If we was to ask nicely.'

Toby's brow furrowed thoughtfully. He really wasn't used to such a barrage of questions. 'Well, I don't know as he'd like you doing that,' he finally managed.

'This town got a marshal?' Dumont suddenly rasped.

The liveryman's face registered amazement. 'A marshal! Now why would we need one of those? Saskatoon's been dry since it opened for business. No drink, no trouble. And *if* there was any,' he added, gazing pointedly at the two Metis. 'Well, then someone would fetch the Mounted Police.'

Mounted Police were the last people on Hatcher's mind. Gawping at Toby in amazement, he exclaimed. 'No whiskey! You've got to be joshing me!'

Brin Carson was tiring of all this palaver. Producing a shiny American Single Eagle from his pocket, he brandished the gold coin in front of Toby's nose enticingly.

'Let's just cut to the chase, old man. Are you gonna fulfil our needs, or do we take our business elsewhere?'

Toby couldn't remember the last time he'd been offered a solid gold coin ... probably because he never had. All resistance faded away with the sight of its lustrous promise, although he did offer a whispered observation of sorts. 'Mister Harriman ain't gonna like it when he finds out their kind have been

107

in his livery.'

Carson favoured him with a cold smile. 'Maybe so, but by the time he finds out, we'll be long gone.'

It was obvious when uttering that, that he wasn't aware of the saying 'famous last words'!

Tector Parsons regarded his fearsome employer warily. As that man had surmised, Parsons had indeed been consorting with a lewd woman and hadn't relished being interrupted. Then again, nobody in his right mind would ignore a summons from Lash Breckenridge. His lethal impatience was common knowledge, so much so that he had pretty much permanently eschewed the use of his lengthy surname, preferring instead to always being known simply as Lash. Its brutal connotations no doubt also appealed to him.

'You took your damn time!' Lash snapped, regarding his subordinate belligerently. Then, in a slightly milder tone, he continued with, 'I've got a job for you,' and briefly related the tale of four intriguing strangers arriving in town. As he spoke, he regarded his employee steadily and unblinkingly. Parsons, in his opinion, was a lazy degenerate, with an excessive fondness for infected 'Dutch gals' and strong drink . . . but he was also loyal, surprisingly good with a gun and possessed at least half a brain. 'So I want you to mosey on down to the livery and see what's cooking. If they happen to get that strongbox open, you be sure an' tell me, pronto!' And with that, he dismissed him with a jerk of the head.

Tector Parsons was, if anything a touch more intelligent than his cynical boss gave him credit for. He had no intention of just wandering into the livery without first seeing what he was getting himself into, whatever Lash Breckin ... Breckon ... whatever his damn name was said! So instead of going straight there, he drifted casually along the street until he was opposite the large premises, and then ducked into a narrow alley between two buildings. Ensconced in the shadows, he was then in a good position to see without being seen.

The gunhand didn't have long to wait. First of all he observed one of the young stablehands accompanying Saskatoon's answer to a doctor into the livery. Parsons' thin lips twisted into a smirk. Doc Barlow was a physician in name only, and more suited to pulling teeth than saving lives. They had barely vanished inside before the same young man reappeared, this time leading a complete stranger. With his tied-down gun and searching gaze, the man looked like some kind of hardcase from south of the border.

The two of them headed directly for Harriman's smithy. Having been informed of the strongbox, Parsons nodded his understanding. Tools for breaking and entering! Therefore, the time to make his apparently casual entrance was once they had returned. That way, no one would come up behind him unawares. Nodding with satisfaction, he settled down on his haunches to wait.

Lash Breckenridge stood behind the substantial counter in his general store. As so often was the case, he was lost in thought, but that mattered little because he employed two clerks to attend to the casual needs of Saskatoon's citizens. He reserved his attention for more important issues, and surprisingly these didn't even include the mysterious strongbox in the stables as yet. That could wait until he had more definitive information. He was far more concerned with a certain high value consignment that was considerably overdue.

The incongruity of his particular situation never failed to bring a wry smile to his brutalised features. The fact that he was running an illicit whiskey trading operation out of a temperance community took some beating. Saskatoon's high and mighty founder, John Lake, had his head so far up his own ass that he appeared oblivious to what was happening right under his nose. With the physical impossibility of that colourful description lost on him, his smile faded as he pondered the likely whereabouts of his three wagonloads of whiskey again. As before, the cargo was destined for Saskatchewan's relatively tame Indians, but first it had to reach him . . . so that it could be watered down and so increase his profit even more.

For some reason, an unpleasant thought began to gnaw away at him. What if unforeseen complications in the livery rebounded on his long-made plans? He recalled the stranger's hard expression. It had been the face of someone used to trouble. Perhaps, after all, it would be best to recall Parsons and forget the whole thing. And yet, the possibility of substantial gain held him in its fateful grip, and he made no move.

The screaming began just as the stranger and the stablehand returned with an assortment of the absent Mister Harriman's tools. The fact that the American didn't even break step meant that he had obviously expected such noise, which, of course, implied that Doc Barlow was extracting far more than just teeth. The commotion would make an ideal distraction for when Parsons entered the livery, supposedly to check on his horse.

Waiting until the two figures had gone inside, he clambered to his feet, loosened his Colt in its holster, and then ambled across the street. The big doors had been closed, but that did little to dampen the God-awful noise coming from within. Grunting, he pulled on one of them with his left hand. As it swung open, Lash's stooge sidled inside to find pretty much most of what he had expected taking place.

In the large, open space in front of the various stalls, two very different operations were under way. On the left, a blood-soaked half-breed lay on the floor, while another of the same ilk straddled his body in a vain attempt to control his struggling. In the process of removing yet another lead pellet, a whiskered Doc Barlow was stoically probing a chest wound. The flesh around it was livid and swollen. A high-pitched wail was abruptly cut short by the casual placing of a knife handle between Gaspard's discoloured teeth.

'Anyone would think you'd never been shot before,' Dumont muttered impatiently, completely oblivious to Parsons' presence.

A few yards to the right, two men were huddled over a strongbox, with Toby and his stablehands making up a fascinated audience near by. The American that he'd seen outside had his back to Parsons, and was in the process of tackling a padlock with a hammer and chisel. His companion was hunkered down at a right angle to him, so that one side of his face was visible to the snooper. The briefest of glances was all it took to raise the hackles on the back of his neck.

'You!' Tector Parsons spat out in an involuntary reflex, even as he reached for the gun on his hip.

The combined exclamation and sudden movement unleashed an instinctive reaction in Brin Carson that left the onlookers stunned. In seemingly one fluid action, he pivoted on his heels, and then drew, cocked and fired his revolver. That first bullet slammed into the intruder before his gun had even cleared leather. Keeping his forefinger tightly on the trigger, and using the heel of his left hand to fan the hammer, the outlaw emptied three more chambers into the luckless Parsons. That man was already dead, but his body jerked like a marionette under the force of the hot lead. With blood drenching the cotton shirt, the corpse fell back against the stable door and then crumpled to the hard-packed earth.

The sudden volley of shots captured everyone's attention, including the doctor and even his patient. Gabriel Dumont's speculative gaze moved rapidly from killer to victim and back again. The gunplay had been all the more impressive for being totally unexpected, and he was only now beginning to realize just what this man was capable of.

'Holy shit!' was Toby's muttered contribution. He was gazing at Carson in awe, and quickly began to run off at the mouth. 'It come to me now. I saw you gun down Sam Smalls in Abilene. It was something to behold. Just like this. You sure ain't slowed down any. In fact you just might could be a touch faster. Wowwee!'

Carson completely ignored his diminutive admirer. With two bullets left, he searched the interior for any more potential threats. It seemed mighty strange that only the one individual had come against them. 'Check outside,' he snapped at his partner, who quickly did as instructed.

'No sign of trouble,' Hatcher reported. 'But there's some mighty puzzled folks out there. Just who the hell was this, anyhu? Somebody's husband?'

'No, somebody's brother,' Carson replied as he replaced the empty cartridge cases swiftly. 'His name's Tector Parsons. I had the pressing need to kill Hector Parsons a few years ago.'

Despite the circumstances, Vern Hatcher guffawed loudly. '*Tector and Hector.* You got to be joshing me!'

113

Carson wasn't in the mood for banter. 'No. No I ain't. But the question is, did he spot me riding in to town and decide to try his hand, or was he sent in here by someone else?'

Whatever the reason behind it, the bloody outcome had had a profound effect on Doc Barlow. 'We haven't seen many gunshot wounds around here ... until you fellows arrived,' he stated accusingly, before staring at Dumont. 'I've extracted the last piece of shot. You don't need me to bandage him. Just pay me in coin and I'll be gone.'

The Metis appeared startled, but not so Carson. That man swung his reloaded revolver over to cover the so-called physician. 'You ain't going anywhere, mister, and neither are the rest of you,' he added for the benefit of the stablehands. 'All we have to do is open this goddamn box an' then you won't see us for dust.' Abruptly focusing his hard eyes on Barlow, he added, 'So get him patched up and ready to ride. Savvy?'

That man swallowed uncomfortably, before reluctantly nodding.

'You youngsters see to our horses,' the American barked, and after ensuring that they were doing exactly that, he then turned to his partner. 'We've got work to do, yeah?'

'Yeah,' Hatcher replied, and together they again closed in on the strongbox.

As the outlaws got to their knees in front of it like a pair of supplicants, a moment of relative calm settled over the livery's interior. It was only then that they first heard a distant clattering noise. As moments passed, that sound grew louder and louder until the thud of hoofs also became apparent. And then men's voices, loud and course, joined in. *And* the whole shebang appeared to be heading directly for the livery.

'For Christ's sake,' Carson raged as he let the hammer slip from his grasp. 'What the hell is it *now*?'

CHAPTER TEN

Lash Breckenridge heard the flurry of gunshots, muffled but nevertheless evident, and instinctively recognized their source immediately.

'What the hell have you gone and done, Tector?' he muttered gloomily to himself.

Rapidly striding to the threshold of his store, Lash peered over at the livery building. There was no further gunplay, but a door opened and one of the four strangers peered around cautiously. Presumably seeing only bemused onlookers, that individual then ducked back inside.

'Shit!' The big man was momentarily stumped. Whatever had taken place in there sure didn't bode well. Yet if Parsons had been paroled to Jesus so swiftly, then it pretty much confirmed that the sons of bitches in the livery had to be in possession of something mighty valuable. Something they would kill to keep. So what Lash needed was more men . . . and fast. With an abrupt lack of customers in his store, he rounded on one of the idle clerks.

'Go find Brett. Tell him to round up any others that he can find and get over here, pronto.'

As the man rushed off, Lash took another look down the street, and it was then that he first heard the sounds that he had been expecting for many a day. Three heavily laden freight wagons were approaching Saskatoon, bringing the chance of vast profits. For a brief moment his spirits soared . . . until the *exact* destination of the latest arrivals dawned on him.

'Shit!' he exclaimed again. Harriman's Livery was the only structure in town that could easily accommodate his consignment, the conveyances that carried it, and the animals that pulled the whole shooting match. The whiskey trader had long before come to an agreement with the owner, concerning the occasional but exclusive use of a section of it when required. Unfortunately, the poxy fellow was inconveniently absent, replaced by four obviously dangerous unknowns. And his investment was heading directly into their hands.

'Goddamn it all to hell!' he raged, frustration as much as anger eating at him. Barrelling to the rear of his store, he shoved the remaining startled clerk to one side, snarling, 'Get out of my way!'

Reaching under the counter, Lash grabbed the sawn-off shotgun that permanently resided there and checked the loads. Such was the relatively peaceful nature of the province that it had been a long while since he'd needed to even produce such a fearsome weapon. The lead wagon had nearly reached the

117

livery, and he briefly debated whether to hurry over alone and head them off. Then he recalled the rapid gunshots, and decided to await reinforcements. Thankfully, they were not long in coming.

Brett Towns, one of the merchant's permanent employees, had three men with him. All were specifically engaged to handle the whiskey trade, and so were conveniently in town awaiting just this shipment. In an earlier and far more violent time, in what had been known as 'Bleeding Kansas', they would have been referred to as border ruffians. Brutalized by life, they did not shrink from resorting to casual violence when necessary . . . and they were about to be told it was.

Lash decided to be economical with the truth, and so carefully omitted certain information. 'The whiskey's finally arrived at the livery,' he rasped. 'Problem is, there's some saddle bums in there who've just up and killed Tector without so much as a by your leave. I don't know what he was doing over there, or why they're here and who they are, but if they get hold of that shipment then you're all out a shitload of *dinero*. So we need to get over there and protect what's ours. Savvy?'

Oh, they savvied all right! With features hard and set, the four of them rapidly checked their assorted firearms. One Colt, one Remington, and two sturdy British Adams, the latter serving to remind anyone who might be interested that this was still the land of Queen Victoria. Then, after a cursory glance down at the other end of the street, they headed for the livery

118

with the measured tread of men possessing a deadly purpose. And yet their options were about to get distinctly limited due to the belligerence of Lash's own freighters.

Unaware that their boss was about to make an appearance, the hot and tired wagoners had reined in their mule teams outside Harriman's premises. The lead driver was now heaving open one of the main doors impatiently. He had fully expected the stablehands to have done that on hearing their arrival, because one thing was for sure: three wagons full of illicit whiskey couldn't be left on the street for some Queen's Cowboy to trip over. The sight that greeted him certainly gave him pause. Three complete strangers had their holster guns aimed directly at him. As was becoming usual, it was Brin Carson who had the words.

'Don't make this more than it is, friend. All we want is to be left alone for a spell, and then we'll be on our way. So you just mosey on back outside, and close the door on your way.'

The burly freighter was obviously not easily intimidated, because he held his ground. 'You must not know who we are, mister. 'Cause if you did, you wouldn't be pointing those shooting irons at me.' But then, as he peered around the interior, his curious gaze took in Doc Barlow and the wounded Metis, and finally settled on Parsons' blood-soaked corpse. His bushy eyebrows rose in stunned surprise. 'Holy shit! Which one of you pus weasels done for Tector?'

'That'd be me,' Carson remarked softly. 'And I'll overlook the insult, but I ain't gonna tell you agin.'

The freighter now regarded him with something akin to respect, and this time did indeed slowly back out, but not without a final sally. 'Just so's you know, Lash ain't gonna like this. You've been warned.' And then he was gone.

'Who or what is Lash?' Hatcher queried.

Carson snorted dismissively. He'd had a bellyful of impediments. 'I don't know and I don't care,' he retorted. Holstering his six-gun, he picked up the hammer again.

'You don't want to cross *him*,' Toby wheezed. Anxiety was aggravating lungs too long abused by cheap roll-ups. 'He's a big man in these parts . . . in more ways than one.'

The train robber's initial response to that was a vicious, well-aimed blow that entirely removed another padlock. Only four now remained, holding in place the two steel bars that reinforced the strong-box's structure.

'All we need is a few more minutes of peace to finish this and divvy up, and then we can hightail it,' he remarked optimistically. 'Then you all can give this bastard box to Mister Harriman as a keepsake!'

'You in the livery,' Lash bellowed. 'Open these goddamn doors, or face the consequences.' Only a long silence greeted that, and the huge fellow glanced darkly at his companions and then growled like an angry grizzly. 'You hear me, Toby, you old buzzard? I've got wagons here that need to be off the street, as well you know. An' if I *can't* have them inside, then no other sons of bitches deserve considerations. I'll burn you out, and Harriman can be damned!'

In the wooden building, Vern Hatcher peered over at Toby. 'Is he spitting out words just to see where they splatter, or what?'

The old-timer shook his head emphatically, real concern etched on his grizzled features. 'Oh, Lash ain't funning. I know him. He's real mean when he gets mad.'

'That's just dandy,' Hatcher exclaimed as he glanced at his partner. 'So what do you reckon then, Brin?'

That man's jaw tightened, and he drew in a deep breath. Taking another tremendous swing at the box resulted in yet one more lock disintegrating. Then abruptly he dropped the hammer and stood up. 'You know what? I'm all done with running. From lawmen or anyone else.' Gazing at Gabriel Dumont, he added, 'Considering as how this is your country, you're awful quiet.'

The Metis glared at the American. He well knew who Lash was, and didn't much want to tangle with him, but that wasn't something he could admit to a pair of damn Yankees. So all he said was, 'I should get Gaspard out through the back. If this place burns, then so will he.'

Carson felt vague niggling suspicion, but couldn't immediately think of an objection. 'Fair enough. You

121

an' the doc get him shifted. Then you cover the rear to make sure no one flanks us.'

Dumont nodded. 'What will you two do?'

Carson favoured him with a mirthless smile. 'Take the fight outside to them bull turds. I ain't figuring on burning to death.' So saying, he bent down and grabbed an unresisting Gaspard's revolver.' Now, with a weapon in each hand, he glanced at his partner and then pointedly at Toby before moving up to the double doors.

There was an asthmatic yelp as Hatcher seized the scrawny stablehand by his neck and thrust him forward. 'Tell them we've seen sense and you're opening up. Any funny business an' you won't see another sunrise. Savvy?'

His eyes like saucers, that man nodded frantically and then yelled out, 'OK, OK, Mister Lash. Please don't start any fires. These fellas don't want no trouble. I'm going to let you in right away.'

The lead freighter was back on his wagon, and Lash gestured for his men to spread out. The long silence had left him deeply suspicious, and yet he really did want his wagons off the street and away from prying eyes.

'I'm coming out. You just hold off now,' Toby continued, and slowly the left-hand door began to open and he stepped into view. What happened next took everyone out front by surprise . . . including Toby!

The hand on his neck shifted to his back, and without any warning he was shoved out into the street and into the path of the nearest mule. Then

Carson and Hatcher erupted from the building at forty-five degree angles, each drawing a bead on the first two men they saw holding guns.

Typically, Carson fired first and most accurately, his bullet striking one of Brett Towns' men just left of centre. The luckless hardcase staggered back, blood gushing from his chest, and his own revolver blasting harmlessly into the dirt. Hatcher was a less proficient gunhand. He snatched his shot, sending the hot lead into a shoulder, but it still served its purpose. The victim spun around under the savage momentum, and then merely stood groggy and disorientated, facing the wrong way and effectively out of the fight.

Rather than killing again, Carson chose to fire his other revolver into the ground . . . right in front of the lead wagon's mule team, and next to the terrified Toby.

'Don't shoot me,' he wailed. 'I ain't done nothing.'

As expected, the combination of gunfire and screaming proved to be too much for the simple beasts. To Lash's absolute horror, they lurched sideways, narrowly missing the hapless stablehand, and hauled the wagon around with such force that it tilted sideways onto two wheels. The mule team behind it, also frightened by the mayhem, pulled sharply away from the continued shooting. The corner of their wagon struck the first one side on, catching it on the roll and pitching the whole conveyance onto its side with a tremendous crash. The freighter managed to safely jump clear, but was then deluged by glass fragments and whiskey as bottles of the precious liquid shattered against each other or on the ground.

Lash Breckenridge was almost beside himself with shock. The sudden outbreak of bloody gunplay had taken him by surprise, but this calamity was even worse because it involved financial loss. 'Shoot the bastards,' was all he could manage, but his remaining men were desperately trying to avoid being crushed by the wagons.

As the second team raced out of town at break-neck speed with its precious cargo, Carson and Hatcher nipped smartly back into the livery, completely untouched, and slammed the door shut. They had done well, and yet they were about to discover that Gabriel Dumont had done better!

The three men, mounted on two horses, sat at the edge of town. Because of the slight curvature of the main street, they could hear but not see the mayhem taking place a short distance away.

'I thought it was supposed to be peaceful up here in Canada,' Jesse Bronson remarked drily.

'It was, until some of *your* lowlifes came north of the line,' Samuel Bairstow retorted, before adding with remarkable prescience, 'You could sure do to pass some tough gun laws down there, otherwise there'll be hell to pay in years to come.'

'The good folks of the US of A would never stand for that,' the marshal retorted, genuinely amazed at such a ridiculous suggestion.

John Fraser stared at his two companions in amazement. Men were presumably shooting at and even killing each other in Saskatoon, and yet these two seasoned lawmen were indulging in apparently meaningless banter. 'Shouldn't we at least go in and see what's occurring?' he urged.

'Happen you're right,' Bronson acknowledged. 'But not you.'

'Yeah, this ain't any kind of job for a sodbuster,' the Mountie asserted grimly, before relenting slightly. 'No offence intended, mister.'

'None taken,' Fraser replied with deceptive calm, before suddenly adopting a far harsher tone. 'But if you expect me to stay here, you can both go to hell! I hope and pray, Sergeant, that your wife will survive, but mine definitely didn't. So one way or another I'm coming with you, and the only way to stop me is to shoot me!'

Bairstow glanced at Bronson who nodded. 'He looks pretty made up to me, Samuel. And besides, we sure could use another gun.'

And so it was decided. They would ride in to Saskatoon, and confront whatever awaited them together.

The two Americans glanced around the interior. As expected, the two half-breeds, Doc Barlow and the young stablehands had all gone. Unfortunately, so too had the strongbox.

'Son of a bitch!' Carson snarled. 'I knew he was up to something.'

'Yeah, but he can't have got far,' Hatcher reasoned. 'All the horses are still here, an' that Gaspard fella wasn't exactly fit as a rutting buck.'

Carson shook his head in frustration. They were faced with a serious dilemma. The only way to get their mounts out of the building was through the main doors, which was patently impossible. Then again, without the contents of the strongbox they couldn't leave anyway, because otherwise all their travails and all the killings would have been for nothing.

'Goddamn it all to hell!' he fumed. 'All we can do for now is follow the money. If that Dumont *has* double-crossed us, I'll cut his poxy heart out.'

Together, guns ready, they padded to the back of the livery. As they feared, the small rear door was open and unguarded. Hatcher cautiously peered outside.

'Looks like you'd better get to sharpening your knife,' he remarked. 'The only action's round the front.'

As the two of them emerged from the building, they discovered that Hatcher's statement had been only partially correct. There was indeed a great deal of shouting and cussing on the main street as Lash attempted to exert control over the chaos, but there were more subtle signs of recent activity at the rear.

Directly opposite the door were the makings of a small but neat cemetery. Because Saskatoon was a relatively new community there were few occupants, although it was fair to suppose that after this day's activity there would likely be a sizeable influx. All of the crosses but one were very meagre affairs. It was against the solid, well-made memorial to one of the town's more prosperous citizens that Gaspard had been propped.

'The location must be of great comfort to him,' Carson observed drily as the two Americans approached cautiously.

The ill-used Metis stared up at them through tear-stained, bloodshot eyes. Despite the hurried medical attention, his many wounds were still bleeding badly. His chances of survival appeared slim, and as the old joke went, 'Slim had just left town'. Under the circumstances, there was nothing more that could be done for him had they even wished to.

'Where's Dumont?' Hatcher demanded softly.

Gaspard's head lolled slightly to one side, but he retained enough strength to point at a nearby building.

'And the strongbox?' Carson added.

The half-breed nodded weakly, a slight smile appearing on his haggard features. Apparently aware of his imminent demise, the prospect of hard cash no longer held any appeal.

The two outlaws saw nothing even vaguely amusing about the turn of events. Turning away dismissively, they advanced on the wooden premises cautiously, both very conscious that they could be heading into a trap. They were also aware that a strange and inexplicable silence had suddenly fallen over the main thoroughfare.

'That loudmouth must have been struck dumb,'

Hatcher muttered uneasily.

Reaching a door, they worked smoothly as a team, with one easing it open so that the other could cover the interior with his revolver. In the centre of a small windowless room stood a trestle table, on top of which lay a covered and apparently sealed coffin. A single kerosene lamp had illuminated the sparse premises. Whatever they might have been expecting, it sure wasn't that. And sprawled on the floor next to the casket was an elderly gent clad in a sober suit. Blood trickled from a gash on his head, but he was still breathing.

'Looks like our Metis friend done laid out the undertaker,' Hatcher whispered drolly.

'Hmm, a nice touch to be sure,' Carson murmured. 'Question is, where might he be now?'

128

CHAPTER ELEVEN

Samuel Bairstow reined in a short distance from the stables and carefully scrutinised the scene before him. His keen gaze took in the overturned wagon, the shattered bottles, and the dead and injured men. Even a blind man on a galloping horse could not miss the fact that something was badly wrong in Saskatoon. The question was, did any of it relate to the men that they were seeking? There was really only the one way to find out.

'This might not involve the sons of bitches that we're chasing,' he remarked, glancing over at Bronson. 'So you might want to stay out of this.'

'You can go to hell in a handcart, my friend,' that man retorted. 'I'm a lawman, same as you. Where I come from that counts for something.'

The Mountie smiled appreciatively. He had expected nothing less. 'Well, I thank you for that,' he replied, before switching his attention quickly to Bronson's passenger. 'But the same doesn't apply to you, sodbuster. You know what we're really here for, so why not take a look around? See what you can turn up. Just stay clear of the carnage over yonder.'

Fraser stared hard at him for a moment before nodding. 'Fair enough, but my name is John Fraser, *not* sodbuster, and I'll be grateful if you would remember that in future.' With that, he slid off the back of Bronson's horse and moved quickly into the nearest alley.

The two lawmen dismounted, tied up their animals on a hitching rail and, keeping a few feet apart, walked steadily towards the disturbance. Their shotguns were cocked and canted across their right shoulders, ready for instant deployment. As they approached the livery, a strange silence fell over the area. Even the mule teams temporarily ceased their braying. A huge fellow with a shotgun of his own was watching them intently. He must have spotted their arrival some minutes before, and had obviously come to his own conclusions about the inconvenient presence of a Mounted Policeman at such a juncture.

'This ain't a good time for an official visit, Sergeant,' he rasped. 'It would behove you to ride on by until another day. You sure won't be the loser by it, if you take my meaning.'

It was Bronson who answered that. 'Seems like things haven't been going your way, mister,' he remarked laconically. 'And from where I'm standing, they're only gonna get worse.'

Lash glared at him menacingly. 'Just who the hell are you?'

The marshal's eyes narrowed slightly, and then the

iron hook tugged his jacket back just enough to display the small medieval shield with a five-pointed star at the centre that was pinned to his chest. 'Jesse Bronson, Deputy United States Marshal.'

Lash blinked in surprise. 'You're a bit off your turf, ain't you, *law dog*?'

'He's with me,' Bairstow snapped. 'And that's all that matters, because I've got jurisdiction over everybody and everything in this province. Now you and your men lower all those shooting irons to the ground. You've got some hard questions to answer, an' I really don't see how you can avoid being in a shitload of trouble . . . seeing as how this is a dry town and it's against the law to sell *any* liquor to the Indians.'

Lash licked suddenly parched lips. As if he didn't have enough to worry about, he'd earlier seen a third man split off from these sons of bitches, and so was troubled by that individual's identity and whereabouts. His head was literally beginning to hurt. He didn't know what he'd done to deserve this sudden downturn in fortune. The fact that he had started it all by sending Tector Parsons on a greed-inspired mission completely escaped him. All he did know was that the removal of these latest interlopers would at least allow him to turn a profit on the remaining whiskey. The wagon that had raced out onto the plains would undoubtedly return once the freighter had regained control of his team. And yet . . . the killing of a Mountie and his companions was one hell of a thing to contemplate. Such a dark deed could

131

not be kept quiet, and would certainly lead to a whole detachment of Mounted Policemen descending on him like the wrath of God. Unless, of course, the murders could be blamed on someone else!

Unfortunately for the scheming whiskey runner, there were now far too many different elements on the loose in Saskatoon. It had only taken an unbelievably short time for him to effectively lose control of a very cushy situation.

John Fraser could make no claim to second sight, but somehow he just knew that his wife's killer was close by. The problem with such knowledge was that when coupled with a complete lack of martial experience, his thirst for vengeance rendered him very vulnerable indeed.

Having reached the end of the alley he turned right, so that his path took him parallel with the main street and along the back of the livery building. He could hear voices round the front of it, but just couldn't quite make out what they were saying. So intent was he on listening that he completely ignored the small cemetery to his left. Then a sudden movement registered in the corner of his vision and his heart quite literally missed a beat as he swung his shotgun around.

A combination of shock and relentless blood loss had finally ended Gaspard's short life. The half-breed's head had tipped forward, so that a blood-coated chin now rested on his chest. For a long moment, Fraser stared at the fresh cadaver with

morbid fascination. The sight of death was something he had not yet got used to, and strangely
enough he felt no satisfaction from this particular
one. Perhaps it was because this was not the man that
he was seeking, which meant that he had to keep
looking, and surely the miserable rogue couldn't be
far away.

As it turned out, it was Gabriel Dumont who insti-
gated the massive eruption of violence that engulfed
Saskatoon that day. Having cautiously vacated the
unfortunate undertaker's front office, he again
found himself on the main street, but set back from
the far larger livery building. By veering off to his
left, the half-breed positioned himself barely around
the corner of the funeral parlour. From that angle he
could just see Lash's massive figure and then beyond
him Bairstow's scarlet tunic. It was then that native
cunning came into play. Why not get the two factions
fighting amongst themselves?

On the way out of the stables, Dumont had
retrieved the Winchester from its leather scabbard
on his horse. Levering a cartridge into the breech, he
took careful aim at the unsuspecting policeman.
Surprisingly, he didn't want Bairstow dead yet, just
riled up. Momentarily holding his breath, the Metis
squeezed the trigger and then ducked back out of
sight without waiting to see the result. There was
little point. He could do nothing about the telltale
powder smoke, and so quite simply his deadly
scheme had either worked or it hadn't.

133

Pretty much as planned, the bullet struck Samuel Bairstow in the meaty part of his left shoulder, gouging through muscle and scoring bone, before ending up in the front wall of Doc Barlow's small premises. Even through the pain and shock, the Mountie instinctively knew that the projectile hadn't come from any of the men before him, but unfortunately that didn't apply to his companion.

Jesse Bronson stood further to the left, and so the funeral parlour was completely out of his line of sight. All he knew was that some son of a bitch had shot his partner, and that these whiskey peddlers could quite easily be in league with the train robbers who were most likely still in town. All of which meant that the two lawmen were heavily outnumbered, and therefore entitled to utilize lethal force.

Pitching the sawn-off forward onto his outstretched left arm, he identified the nearest potential threat, which just happened to be Brett Towns. That man saw what was coming and reached for his belt gun, thereby effectively sealing his own fate. Rather than going for the legs, the marshal opted for a kill shot and emptied a barrel into Towns' chest. The full load tore into flesh and blood, throwing the man backwards off his feet. With a resounding thump, he hit the dirt and lay twitching in his death throes, blood pumping from the fatal wound.

'Jesus Christ!' bellowed Lash. He'd heard the rifle shot behind him, but hadn't the faintest idea who had fired. And now, faced with two apparently kill-crazy lawmen, it really didn't matter.

134

Bairstow, hurting badly but still on his feet, levelled his own shotgun at the big man. And yet he didn't immediately fire. He was trained to uphold the law, not shoot on sight, and the men before him hadn't started this. Yet in reality he recognized that it was far too late for such niceties, because the damage had been done.

Lash Breckenridge had a lot of hard bark on him, but basically he was a merchant gone rogue rather than an experienced man-killer. Faced with two sawn-offs in the hands of professionals, his resolve weakened. Twisting away, he ran with the speed of desperation for the relative safety of the overturned wagon. Crunching through a sea of broken glass, he slipped on a patch of whiskey-sodden dirt and went crashing down. The sudden fall undoubtedly saved his life, because it was at that instant that Bairstow triggered his big gun.

The hail of shot slammed into timber rather than flesh, but Lash certainly didn't get away unscathed. Shards of wet glass punctured his arms and legs, causing his trigger finger to contract. Both barrels of his shotgun discharged into the wagon bed, sending a blizzard of wood splinters in all directions.

'Bastard!' he howled as he frantically scrambled for cover.

Lash's remaining 'heavy', together with the two freighters, both armed from their journey across the plains, gazed askance at both Towns' blood-soaked corpse and their cowering boss. Simultaneously, they decided that it was probably time to seek new employment. Dropping their weapons as though they were hot coals, they stood with their hands held high.

Bronson spat a stream of tobacco juice into the dirt. 'Wise choice, fellas,' he opined. About to advance, he was stopped in his tracks by Bairstow's sudden warning.

'These pus weasels didn't start this. There's someone back of them who shot me, and for my money it's one of them darned train robbers.'

The marshal pondered for a moment, a trickle of dark juice on his bristly chin. 'Can you stay on your feet for a while longer, so's I can fetch some shackles?'

The Mountie was white-faced but determined. 'Get to it,' he muttered, as he swiftly replaced the spent twelve-gauge cartridge. His scarlet jacket was wet with blood, but from past experience he reckoned it would be some time yet before he fainted.

'All of you get over here,' Bronson ordered. 'An' don't try anything, or this *dis*Mounted Policeman will unload both barrels on you.' With that, he quickly retired to the horses.

Lash staggered painfully to his feet, and began gingerly pulling pieces of glass from his person. 'I'm like to bleed out,' he moaned miserably.

'You and me both, mister,' Bairstow retorted. 'But look at it this way. With the amount of whiskey already in those wounds, they're not likely to infect. Now get over here with the others, or you'll be the worse for it.' He was very aware of at least one other

gunman over yonder somewhere, and so four prisoners would make a useful human shield.

Over beyond the undertaker's, Dumont worked the
under-lever on his Winchester. The engineered set-to
hadn't gone quite as well as intended. He had been
hoping for something approaching mutual destruc-
tion. Sadly, it now appeared as though he'd have to
finish the job himself. Then an all too familiar voice
called out through the thin timber wall.

'That you out there, Dumont?' Brin Carson
demanded. He and his companion were in the
undertaker's front room, which served as an office
and boasted a large, lettered window facing out onto
the street.

'It is I,' the Metis responded. 'We've got a chance
to finish these law dogs once and for all. I've
wounded the redcoat.'

Hatcher had other things on his mind. 'Where's
the goddamn gold, you son of a bitch?'

Dumont sighed loudly. 'In a safe place, Yankee.
Now are you with me or not?'

'Yes, he is,' Carson replied swiftly. 'Thing is, I can't
see the marshal.'

'He's gone for some iron bracelets. As soon as he
comes back, we let him shackle those whiskey peddlers and then blast them all. Yeah?'

'Yeah!'

The hair went up on the back of John Fraser's neck.
Crouching next to the still-unconscious undertaker,

he had overheard most of what had been said. The question was, what could he do about it? As a hero in a dime novel, he would have fearlessly kicked the connecting door open and blasted the two Americans to purgatory with his shotgun. But this was real life, and he was so scared that there was a genuine possibility of him soiling his pants. Then he recalled the way in which Sergeant Bairstow had approached the Cree war party, alone but apparently undaunted. With the memory fixed in his mind, Fraser accepted he just had to do something. That led to a recollection of the dead Metis back in the small graveyard. Perhaps even the departed could come in useful.

Quietly exiting the building, he rushed over to the bloody corpse. Placing his shotgun on the ground, the farmer grimaced with distaste, but nevertheless heaved Gaspard over his right shoulder. Grunting under the literally dead weight, he lurched to his feet and then proceeded unsteadily along the alley between livery and funeral parlour. As he reached the front, his limbs began to tremble from more than just the effort involved. This next bit would involve the most danger. Because of the way the livery building jutted out, he had no idea of Bronson and Bairstow's situation. All he could do was give his all and hope for the best.

Drawing in a deep breath, he tottered around the corner. First there was a door and then the large window. Surging forward past the threshold, Fraser suddenly came to a jarring halt. Heaving with all his might, he launched the cadaver into the sheet of glass.

The two Americans were waiting for Bronson to appear across the street. Until then there was little point in advertising their presence. They were poised, weapons ready, when a dark shape appeared abruptly outside the window and then all hell broke loose. Without any warning, the whole expanse of glass exploded inwards. The body that came with it knocked Vern Hatcher clean off his feet, and brought exactly the reaction from Carson that Fraser had hoped for.

With lightning-fast reactions, the gunhand unleashed three rapid shots into the street, narrowly missing the retreating farmer. Only then, on seeing Gaspard's waxy features, did he realize that they had been suckered.

'What the hell are you shooting at, *imbecile*?' Dumont yelled angrily, but of course by then it was too late.

With the prisoners under Bairstow's gun, Bronson had succeeded in manacling Lash and his surviving thug. About to move on to the two freighters, he was stopped in his tracks by a sudden ruckus down the street. The accompanying gunfire claimed everyone's attention.

The Mountie was incredulous. 'That sodbuster just threw something or someone through a goddamn window.' Even as he spoke, he was moving

139

into the cover of the upturned wagon. And blood loss certainly hadn't affected his thought processes. Gesturing to the two freighters with his shotgun, he commanded, 'Unhitch the team off that other wagon. We might could have use for it, an' all this shooting's like to spook them mules.'

Lash didn't like the sound of that one little bit. 'What you thinking on? Ain't it enough that I'm cut to pieces?'

Bronson jabbed him mighty hard in the belly with his big gun. 'You ain't careful I'll cut you in half with this, *Indian trader*,' he snarled. 'Back down the trail a ways, we came up against a band of liquored up Cree out for our scalps. And but for this policeman they might have got them!'

Lash was doubled over in pain, but even had he been able to speak he would have been drowned out by renewed gunfire from the undertaker's. The outlaws had the two freighters in their sights. Those men had just released the mules, and now leapt for their lives behind the stranded wagon. Their employer could only watch helplessly as his valuable animals raced out of town. For him, the continuing financial pain was worse than the physical, and there was far more to come.

'We try flushing them out of there an' we'll get to dying for sure,' Bronson opined. Peering uncertainly at the weakened Mountie, he asked, 'I know you're hurting, Samuel, but are you up to giving cover with that crowd-pleaser while I set these fellas to work?'

Bairstow nodded grimly. 'What've you got in mind?'

The marshal favoured him with a sly smile before sharing it with the prisoners. 'It's past time those train robbers were brought to heel, an' that wagon'll make a doozy of a battering ram filled with all them bottles and such.'

The dismay on Lash Breckenridge's blood-smeared features was plain for all to see. 'Aw shit!' was really about all he could manage.

CHAPTER TWELVE

With gunfire ringing out behind him, John Fraser returned to the graveyard and recovered his shotgun. It occurred to him that his best course was to stay put, and so cover the rear. That way, if the murdering half-breed survived the lawmen's inevitable assault, he would be perfectly placed to avenge Laura. With his shotgun cocked and ready, the farmer settled down on his haunches behind the wooden cross that had supported the unfortunate Gaspard. If there was one thing that his hard life had taught him, it was the value of patience.

'What the hell are those bastards up to now?' Dumont demanded of the two Americans. He had swiftly joined them through the front door, only to be confronted by his countryman's shocking resting place, covered as he was in shards of glass.

'Never mind them,' Carson snapped impatiently. 'Where's the strongbox?'

The Metis regarded him pityingly. 'If you came in

through the back, you walked right past it. I put it in the casket for safety.'

That tickled Hatcher. 'Haw, haw, haw. A coffin full of dollars! I like it. I like it a lot. But what if someone had buried it?'

His partner completely failed to see the joke. Apart from being naturally obsessive, it hadn't escaped Carson's notice that the box's contents had now to be split only *three* ways. This was shaping up to be the big payday he'd always dreamed of, and thanks in part to the lethal efficiency of their pursuers. 'Well I'll feel a lot happier when it's in here, right next to me,' he remarked gravely, turning to the dividing door.

'Why don't we *all* get it together,' the suspicious half-breed barked, swinging his rifle over. Then across the street, a shotgun suddenly discharged.

'Forget it, both of you,' Hatcher retorted. 'They're on the move out there, and it ain't looking good.'

'D'you realize how much of *my* money I've got tied up in this wagon?' Lash bellowed, some of his old belligerence returning. 'I ain't pushing it anywhere just to get it shot full of holes!'

Bronson and his four prisoners were standing behind the second wagon. Now bereft of its mule team, it would require some considerable, and very reluctant, human muscle power to get it moving. The marshal's eyes glinted dangerously.

'You're kind of forgetting something. It ain't yours anymore, on account of it's been confi . . . confis . . .

seized. So get shoving!'

Three of the men put their shoulders to the rough-cut timber, but the aggrieved trader stubbornly held his ground. The lawman sighed. He hadn't got time for this. Without warning, he lowered his sawn-off and squeezed one trigger. Accompanied by a tremendous roar, *most* of the lead shot blasted into the ground at Lash's feet. But a couple of stray pieces tore into his left boot, bringing a fresh wave of agony to a body that was already hurting bad.

'You miserable son of a bitch!' Lash howled as he hopped on one foot. 'I thought you was a *peace* officer. You nearly blew my goddamn foot off!'

Bronson was completely unperturbed. 'Put your back to that wagon, or the other barrel turns you into a cripple.'

Moaning from a mixture of distress and anger, the big man turned and hobbled over to his former possession. 'Give me some room,' he snarled at the others.

With the four of them now heaving against it, the heavily loaded conveyance began to move slowly across the wide thoroughfare. A noticeable tinkling of bottles in their crates could be heard, as though they were maliciously seeking to remind Lash of their presence. With Bronson following at the rear, the wagon gradually picked up speed. Fully recognizing their peril, the train robbers opened fire with everything they'd got. Bullet after bullet penetrated the front of it, smashing into the full whiskey bottles so that a trail of Lash's amber liquid followed in its wake. To his increasingly addled brain it felt like deliberate torment.

In an attempt to suppress the resistance, Bairstow emptied his shotgun at the funeral parlour, but that only provided temporary respite. It was as he attempted to replace the spent cartridges that he began to feel faint. Knowing that he was no use to anyone on his back, he snatched the kerchief from around his neck and screwed it into a thick pad. Stuffing it under his jacket, he pressed it over the seeping wound. It would have to do. It was all he had.

'Push, goddamn it!' Bronson urged. He deliberately held off from firing his shotgun. There would be time for that in a moment, because the wagon, now moving at a fast walking pace, was barely yards from the building. Those tarnal outlaws were about to get more whiskey than even they could handle.

Through the shattered window, the three men watched the unstoppable juggernaut with frank dismay. They were almost choking on the sulphurous smoke that filled the room, and yet it seemed that all their defensive gunfire was doing was wasting precious cartridges and creating a great deal more broken glass.

'The hell with this!' Dumont yelled. 'We'd need a howitzer to stop that thing. I'm out of here.'

For once, Hatcher agreed with the half-breed. 'He's right, Brin. We've got to make a break for it.'

145

His partner's eyes gleamed feverishly. Very unusually, money was no longer uppermost in his thoughts. 'You two go if you must. Get the box and wait out back. Me, I ain't running any more. I want to kill me that damn marshal so bad!'

'Don't be a fool,' his friend protested, placing a hand on the other's shoulder. 'We can still make it out of here *and* be rich.'

'I said *git*,' Carson bellowed, shaking him off, and cocking his revolver in readiness.

Hatcher and Dumont glanced at each other and collectively shrugged. Neither had any liking for the other, but they did have one thing in common: a strong desire to stay alive. So, with no more ado, they fled into the back room. The undertaker, gradually coming to, had just struggled into a sitting position. As the two men reached the coffin, they wrenched the lid off and unceremoniously threw it at him. Unable to defend himself, he accepted another blow to the head and sank back to the floor of his premises.

'It really ain't his day,' Hatcher chuckled as he reached in to seize one side of the strongbox. It was at that moment that an earthquake seemed to strike the building.

Despite his belligerence, Brin Carson fell back at the sight of the massive conveyance as it mounted the wooden sidewalk and ploughed into the parlour's front. After all, he wanted to kill, not be killed. With a tremendous rending crash, the whole

146

wall disintegrated like matchwood under the unstoppable assault, and with it went most of the ceiling. Throwing himself to one side, the gunhand *just* got out of the vehicle's path. With a little more momentum, it would have carried on into the back room. As it was, it ground to a halt mere inches from Carson's legs. There he lay, covered in dust and splinters, waiting for someone to shoot at.

The four men behind the wagon had the sense to stay put. Although full of glass, its great bulk at least offered some protection. Jesse Bronson, however, didn't have that luxury. He had fugitives to apprehend. Ducking to one side, he fired his shotgun into the interior, and almost died in the process. A bullet slammed into the wagon side bare inches from his head. With a splinter suddenly lodged painfully in his right cheek, he swore vehemently. His own spread of lead shot had merely peppered the wrecked building harmlessly. Whoever remained inside was well hidden under the wreckage.

Glancing at his now superfluous prisoners, the marshal barked, 'Get the hell away from here unless you've got a death wish.' Then he bellowed back to his wounded companion. 'Are you up to watching these pus weasels, Samuel?'

'Yeah, I guess,' came the weary, but determined retort.

Three of the four men silently backed off, but Lash regarded him with great suspicion. 'What the hell are you fixing on doing?' he demanded angrily.

Bronson favoured him with a bloody grimace.

'Like I keep telling you, mister, this bug juice ain't yours anymore. And since I couldn't drink it all in one sitting, I might as well put it to good use.' With that, he cradled the shotgun, pulled a Lucifer from his pocket and struck it against the rough-cut timber. 'Back up or burn, you big oaf.' So saying, he tossed the burning stick onto a pool of whiskey that had collected under the wagon.

Even with high alcohol content, hard liquor was surprisingly flame-resistant, but after being confined in glass bottles under a hot sun for many hours the vapour from the Indian trader's product was more than ready to ignite. The flames began under the vehicle, but quickly spread to all four corners of it. Lash could only shake his head in uncharacteristically mute despair and walk back to join the others. It really wasn't his day!

Bronson replaced the spent shotgun cartridge and watched as the blaze spread to the building, and more seriously up into the wagon bed. There were still a lot of unbroken bottles in there, and so reluctantly he too retreated a few paces. With shattered wood from the collapsed roof now catching fire, the heat inside the undertaker's was growing intense, far too much for human flesh to withstand.

Bursting up from the wreckage, Brin Carson hollered out, 'You miserable cockchafer,' and opened up a rapid fire at the rear of the wagon.

The marshal waited until he heard dry firing, and then stepped sharply to one side and squeezed both triggers. With seemingly one tremendous detonation, both chambers blasted forth their deadly loads. The full spread tore into Carson's unprotected body, throwing him back against the dividing door. Even if he'd still been alive, no help would have been forth-coming from beyond it, because his two cronies had other things on their minds.

Even before the flames took hold, Hatcher and Dumont had tacitly agreed that Carson was a lost cause, which meant that the money now only had to be split *two* ways. Together they lifted the coveted strongbox out of the coffin and headed for the rear door. Then the American got wind of the conflagra-tion, and more particularly the sickly sweet smell of burning flesh, as flames seared Gaspard's body. He glanced down at the unmoving undertaker. Vern Hatcher had never baulked at murder in his time, but there was something rather pathetic about the prone old man that surprisingly gave him pause.

'It just don't seem right letting this old coot burn to death,' he announced abruptly. 'You haul the box outside while I drag him over to his cemetery.' Lowering his side to the floor, he then took hold of their victim under the shoulders and heaved. The sound of rapid firing followed by the deeper report of a shotgun infused him with fresh energy.

Shrugging dismissively, the half-breed pulled open the door and dragged his far more valuable load outside. Catching sight of the flames around the front, he decided that the graveyard was also proba-bly the best place for him, and so turned to face his destination. Unfortunately, what he saw there gave him no comfort at all!

'You butchered my wife!' John Fraser bellowed, raw emotion almost overwhelming him. The words sounded strange to his ears, as though uttered by someone else. His forefinger tightened, but something held back the ultimate pressure.

It's a hell of a thing to kill a man, and until recently Fraser had had very limited experience of violence. Then Gabriel Dumont foolishly lifted his Winchester, and self-preservation kicked in. A mixture of fear and anxiety meant that the farmer jerked back on the triggers, causing the long barrelled shotgun to fire high. Yet at such close range that really didn't matter. The devastating blast completely obliterated Dumont's swarthy features, turning his flesh into chopped meat, and throwing him back inside the building. The ruined half-breed landed directly in Hatcher's path. That man grimaced at the gory sight, but sidestepped and continued dragging his unconscious load clear of the doomed building.

Out in the open, the outlaw stared pointedly at Fraser and at the smoke curling from *both* barrels of his long gun. 'You've had your two and got your man, mister. So I reckon I'll just take this box and be on my way. Don't make me have to kill you.' With that, he released his hold on the hapless undertaker, and so as to keep his gun hand free began to haul the strongbox towards the back door of the livery with only his left.

The farmer just stared at him numbly. It hadn't yet sunk in that he'd finally, and so totally, annihilated Laura's murderer. He really had no interest in this other piece of saddle trash. And yet suddenly it was no longer his problem.

'The only place you're headed is the Manitoba Penitentiary,' Jesse Bronson remarked conversationally. He had removed the painful splinter in his cheek, cleansed the wound with one of the many bottles of whiskey available, and then homed in on the sound of the shotgun blast. 'Sergeant Bairstow says it's got quite a reputation, whatever that means. Although, if it's proven that you kilt that fireman on the train, then you'll surely hang.'

Vern Hatcher sighed and turned to face the marshal. That individual's sawn-off was aimed directly at him. 'You don't give a man much slack, do you, Bronson? Don't it count for anything that I saved that old gravedigger?'

The lawman's nose twitched and he shrugged. 'You're alive, ain't you? Besides, there ain't gonna be much call for his kind today. Cremation seems to be right popular in these parts.'

The fire had now spread to the whole building and the heat was intense. Gesturing with his shotgun, Bronson ordered, 'Get your right hand in the air. Then, using your left hand, unbuckle that gun belt and toss the whole rig over yonder. And anything else you've got on you that could kill.'

Hatcher's shoulders slumped slightly as he complied. It occurred to him that life really could be ass-wiping bad sometimes.

'Now, shift that strongbox over towards the livery,' Bronson continued remorselessly. 'It's getting hot as Hades here.'

Hatcher sighed again, long and deep. 'At least let me see what all this was about, for Christ's sake. We've drug this damn box across half of Canada!'

As he moved away into less super-heated air, the marshal chuckled slightly. 'Huh, well I guess there's no harm in it. I'm kind of curious to see what's in there myself. Sodbuster . . .' Then he recalled something. '*Mister John Fraser*, would you be good enough to fetch a hammer or some such from the livery?'

That man nodded vaguely as though in a dream, but nevertheless complied swiftly enough. Only moments later he was back with a hammer.

'You stole it, you open it,' the lawman barked at Hatcher.

His woes momentarily forgotten, the train robber got to work with a will. For a few frenetic moments he smashed away at the heavy padlocks, until finally the last one dropped away. The steel bars that had encased the strongbox lay in the dust. It had been a long time coming, but at last he was in. Almost reverently, he lifted the lid. It creaked loudly, but no longer resisted. Inside was a number of bulging canvas bags, their necks tightly fastened by drawstrings. The legend *Canadian Pacific Railroad* was inscribed in black on each of them. Hatcher hefted one. My, but it was heavy.

'Hee, hee,' was all he could manage.

'Use that cutting tool in your boot to open one . . . carefully,' Bronson suggested, proving that he still didn't miss a trick.

Hatcher was too excited to register dismay at being caught out. He just pulled the concealed knife and sliced through the cord gleefully. Even Fraser crowded in, anticipation writ large on his features. At that precise moment, the blazing building and all the killings abruptly counted for nothing. Tearing open the neck of the bag, the outlaw theatrically upended its contents into the box lid. As the *cash* spilled out, elation turned to confusion. Then, despite the heat, his body went cold all over. They were like no gold coins he'd ever seen before, and why the hell did they have holes in the middle?

'What in tarnation's all this?' he mumbled in astonishment. His dirt-stained features appeared to have aged ten years in as many seconds.

The sudden voice from beyond the strongbox's orbit took everyone by surprise. 'Them's washers. I understand they have many uses, but spending's not one of them.'

Samuel Bairstow smiled understandingly at the momentary confusion on his fellow lawman's features. 'You've met my inspector. You couldn't expect him or any above him to risk losing another box of specie to this pus weasel and his cronies. As it is, there's nothing lost, and everything gained.'

Bronson chuckled. 'Well I'll be a son of a . . .'

'My wife was lost!' John Fraser wailed. 'And for what?'

'The contents of that box wouldn't have changed anything,' the Mountie answered sadly. 'And for all I know Kirsty could be . . . Where's Dumont?'

Fraser indicated the burning building. 'In there.'

Bairstow nodded with grim satisfaction. 'That'll do.'

Before anyone could say anything else, they were interrupted by a sudden commotion on the main street. The third and only surviving whiskey wagon had returned, and was wheeling around in front of the livery. Bronson, for one, guessed what that portended, and after a swift inspection of the ashen-faced Mountie decided that he would have to be the one to react. Carefully placing his shotgun on the ground, he glanced at the farmer.

'Reckon you can get me that Winchester?'

Dumont's long gun lay where it had fallen after he'd been shot. It was uncomfortably close to the conflagration, and so the marshal pulled a single leather glove from his jacket. Even with that on, he could feel the intense heat from the metalwork as Fraser tossed it into his grasp. It was a wonder that the cartridges hadn't cooked off.

'Keep an eye on our prisoner,' he said to Bairstow and then headed back to the main street.

He arrived there in time to see Lash Breckenridge and his three employees hurriedly leaving town aboard the wagon. The big man was on the bench seat next to his driver, who was desperately whipping more speed out of his tired mule team. The others were crouching precariously on top of the prized cargo.

Cocking his overheated Winchester, Bronson fired once into the air, before bellowing after the fugitives. 'The next one's a kill shot. Turn that wagon around or face the consequences.'

The reaction to that was surprising. The driver literally threw the reins at his boss and leapt off the wagon. Likewise with the passengers in the rear, who ended up sprawled in the grass. Two of them were obviously in pain from breaks or sprains. That left only Lash, still manacled and heading north with everything he had remaining in the world.

As he worked the under-lever, the marshal sighed. Shooting a man in the back didn't sit well with him, but he really had no choice, because stopping men in flight came with the job. And every passing moment expanded the distance between them. Raising the ladder sight, Bronson set it for two hundred yards and then rested the forestock on his iron hook. Taking into account movement and a diminishing target, there really was no opportunity to administer a flesh wound. And so, aiming directly at a broad back, he drew in a breath and then squeezed.

The heavy bullet struck the whiskey trader dead centre. Yet for a few seconds, the escape attempt continued apparently unchecked. Then Lash's massive frame pitched forward over the wagon's front and down between the two nearest mules. The vehicle bounced slightly as one of the iron-rimmed wheels rolled over and fractured both his legs. It mattered not, of course, because by then Mister Breckenridge was already dead.

Bronson grunted unhappily. Such an outcome gave him no great satisfaction. He watched as, without a driver, the heavily laden wagon gradually ran out of steam. The sodbuster could have the dubious pleasure of bringing that back to town, he decided.

Lash's three employees, one of whom was still shackled, peered at him warily from where they had landed.

'You fellas might as well scat,' the lawman remarked. 'I ain't got any interest in you today.'

'But I done broke my arm,' one of them protested.

'Then it's lucky for you there's a sawbones in town,' Jesse Bronson retorted. 'I reckon you'll be first in line behind the undertaker.' With that, he turned away and slowly made his way back to the others.

EPILOGUE

Kirsty Bairstow, *née* Landers, had been conscious, on and off, for about two days when her husband tentatively entered the cabin. He had already been told that she was miraculously not only still alive but gaining strength, and still couldn't quite believe his . . . *their* good fortune. As they suddenly found themselves staring at each other's features, their mutual happiness was indescribable. Their eyes grew misty from tears of joy. Although still very pale, it was obvious to him that his lovely young wife was on the mend. Moving closer to the bed, he longed to smother her in kisses, but was wary of her fragility. Then, as Kirsty spotted the dried blood on his jacket, her delight rapidly changed to concern.

'Oh, God, you've been fighting again, Samuel.'

The Mountie smiled reassuringly, and then gestured for his companion to come in. 'That usually happens when I'm in company with this rascal, my love.'

Unusually for him, Jesse Bronson was slightly ill at

ease as he joined them. Never having married, and being completely undomesticated, for a few awkward seconds the American was at something of a loss for words. Then Kirsty beamed at him and reached out a hand.

'Get yourself over here and give me a kiss, Marshal, seeing as my brave husband doesn't seem up to the task.'

The grizzled lawman complied happily, leaning over the bed but refraining from embracing her. To his experienced eyes, she still looked pretty damned weak. Then, straightening up, he assumed the tone of a well-meaning scold. 'Now, for Christ's sake, kiss this man of yours. He's been worried sick over you.'

The first traces of colour came to her cheeks. 'One question first. Then he can happily have a thousand kisses. What became of the cowardly cur that shot me?'

For a brief moment, Bronson's expression hardened. 'He got his just reward. Someone sent him to the hot place!'

As the two lawmen stood together, next to the eastbound train at Moose Jaw's railroad depot, Jesse Bronson willingly accepted Samuel Bairstow's warm handshake. The latter had managed to tear himself away from his wife long enough to see the marshal off. Because of the vagaries of the American and Canadian railroad systems, it wasn't simply a matter of heading southwest. Yet no matter how many stop offs were involved, the journey would still be far quicker, and a damned sight easier, than riding horseback all the way to Billings, Montana.

'It's been a pleasure, Samuel,' Bronson announced affectionately. 'You really are fine people. It's just a crying shame you still haven't been paid yet, ha ha. Anyhu, you take good care of yourself and that little lady.'

'Likewise,' was the Mountie's economical response. He would have been loath to admit the fact, but he was genuinely choked up at the American's departure, and was relieved to be able to switch over to more practical matters. 'Inspector Longshanks telegraphed with orders to thank you for helping stop the train robberies and also the whiskey peddlers. All of a sudden, he's quite impressed with the US Marshals Service.' Then he glanced at Bronson's companion, and a chill came over his features. 'Don't let this trash give you any trouble, you hear?'

As a courtesy to the Northwest Mounted Police, the marshal had agreed to escort a particularly important prisoner for part of his journey. Vern Hatcher was feeling more than a little aggrieved. Heavy iron shackles secured both his wrists and ankles, with additional chains connecting the two sets. All movement was both severely restricted and noisy, so that even something as simple as walking was thoroughly unpleasant.

'You must think I'm a real dangerous *hombre*, Marshal,' he muttered sourly.

'No, not really,' the lawman retorted dismissively.

'Only I've never yet lost a prisoner, an' I ain't about to start now.' Finally parting company with Bairstow, he none too gently shoved Hatcher towards the carriage steps, adding, 'And something else for you to chew on. Don't even *think* about trying to rob this train!'